LIAR LIAR

J. A. WINTERS

LIAR LAIR

Editing by: Spell bound editing

Interior Formatting: Dawn Lucous, Yours Truly Book Services

TO ALL THE BEAUTIFUL MONSTERS

It is amazing how complete is the delusion that beauty is goodness — Leo Tolstoy

Lies.

The foundation of any good relationship.

Now, before you go shaking your head and tearing my throat out, listen to what I have to say. I know you'll find some truth in my reasoning.

There are different kinds of lies – fifty fucking shades of ways to twist the truth – and behind each one, lies a reason. Not all are devious, not all are treacherous, and some are designed to save your feelings.

Lies can save you in an unforeseen situation, help you get the girl or seal a deal. There are only consequences if you get caught.

So don't.

The truth is that life is a numbers game. You just need to know how to play them, how to work the system in your favour.

The thing about me? I'm not a liar. Not in the way that I weave intricate tales I would later have to remember. I have my lines, my simple go-to untruths when I'm picking up and need to disappear. The secret of a good lie is to keep it simple, don't complicate things, don't give too many details.

And always, always have an escape plan.

BEFORE

DORIAN

We all eat lies when our hearts are hungry.

I slick my coal-black hair into place and straighten my tie, then continue to admire myself in the mirror. It's not hard. I'm a good-looking guy. The gods have blessed me with incredible genes; sharp jawline, high cheekbones, and green eyes that have been compared to emeralds and deep forests by sweet girls who've drowned in them. I'm 6'5, broad-shouldered and in immaculate shape. I've been called an arrogant asshole, but that's because people who do not understand perfection are jealous. And yes, I am perfect. I am a flawless specimen. Every inch of me is created to induce a reaction from you. For the most part, if you're another man, you will feel inadequate, envious, and threatened, and then you will try to emulate me because, let's face it, everyone wants to be closer to greatness.

But women?

Their breaths will catch in their throats and their eyes will remain glued to my face. Should I look at them, their cheeks will stain pink, and they'll giggle uncomfortably in a strange state of panic and embarrassment. In women I incite infinite desire and immediate trust. My words twist around their overwhelmed little brains, and every word I say persuades them to do my bidding.

It's not my fault these lesser specimens react to me as they do, and I'm not going to lie, the effect I have on them brings me great pleasure, and sometimes, if I give enough shits, them too.

I lick my lips and step out of the bathroom ready for another night out.

||||

The bar is an elegant mix of modern and sexy. Dark tones and sharp lines give it a contemporary clean look. It's a place for people like me. Gods amongst men. The elite. I'm not talking about just us good-looking in society, but the overindulgent filthy rich who can afford ridiculous luxuries. That's just the way I designed it when I created it. A haven to keep the misfits out, and a place where my upstairs apartment could be used at any given time without me having to go too far.

I sweep the room. Plenty of sheep to choose from once the mood hits.

Women.

Delicate, soft, and so very fragile. Their minds akin to breaking, easily manipulated and snapped. It's not my fault they reek of desperation. Sometimes in my weak moments, I almost feel sorry for them, but then I remember that I'm a hunter and they are my prey, and if I want to eat, I must conserve energy–it's easier to pick off weaker prey, so I don't allow myself to worry too much. Really, they do it to themselves.

There are three categories of women, and each draws its own challenge. None I can't surpass, of course, but a challenge nonetheless.

The first is those who, like me, have been blessed with stunning good looks. They understand the appeal of a beautiful body and a beautiful face. The attraction is mutual and short-lived, and we both know the night we spend together will only be for gratification.

The problem with these women is that they carry all these convoluted feelings of want. They want more. They want to be seen as more than their outer shell, they want to think they are funny or intelligent or have more to offer. Ninety per cent of the time they don't, but they despair and get desperate and end up with some ugly fucker way out of their league who makes them laugh and follows them around like a soft little puppy.

In category two are the self-enhanced beauties. Those who understand they are nowhere near perfect and require modern medicine to help them achieve a status close to mine. Of course, they never will, but I can appreciate the effort. The over-the-top full lips, the shelf-bought boobs and bottled hair. These girls are willing because they think they've cracked some kind of beauty code and that somehow, they match perfection.

They're fun but noisy, they laugh too loudly and talk too much. They want too much attention. I just want a hole. They think they're worth more cause their bodywork has been heavily modified and worth more than the average car. I like putting them in their place. I like reminding them that anything bought can be returned, including them.

The final category is one I don't often dip into, not because it's beneath me, but because of the consequences. See, these girls are the average, the uglies of society. They come in so many shapes and sizes that often it's a single quality that draws me to them. Natural full lips, or a rounded ass or perfect fucking tits I know will fit perfectly in the palm of my hand. More often than not it's their faces that's the problem, but I guess that's what doggy style is for.

The real issue with these girls is that they're clingers. Once a god like me touches them, they think they're special or worthy. They want a phone number and another date. Because of their pathetic desperation to be noticed, to be wanted, to be desired, they are willing to do just about anything you ask of them. They will bend their bodies into unnatural shapes, open their throats till they choke and gag, bleed through their ass just to please me. To do my bidding. I have to admit that despite their unfortunate looks they are my favourite flavour. Who wants a vanilla goddess when you can have a kinky whore that tastes like a chocolate Sundae banana split?

I scour the bar sipping on my whiskey. Refined and smooth, like me. I feel eyes on me. It's a given. I'm always watched. Beauty like mine is adored and sought after. I'm okay with the endless looks, the ogling, the admiration., I thrive on it, and it makes everything infinitely easier. Like right now, when her eyes catch mine and I flash her a smile. I know I've just found my chocolate sundae for the night. I'll go test the waters and, if she's up for it, I might get a cherry to put on top of her. I smirk at the idea and her eyes grow rounder on the other side of the room as I rise to my full height and make my way over to her.

She's not what you might label as ugly, but she is on the average side. A little plump, with bright red hair that's not natural but coloured, a deep shiny crimson that flares around her face. Her brown eyes lock on mine and, as I approach, she shifts a little like she's uncomfortable in her own skin. The extra weight will work to my advantage when I pump her ass later and need something to grab onto –

broader girls are easier to hold onto than skinny ones, but what draws me to her are her lips. Those full, thick lips will look incredible wrapped around my cock. It twitches in my pants at the thought.

"Hello." I put my glass down next to hers and encroach on her personal space. She looks to her left as if she's unsure I am addressing her. It's adorable in a stupid kind of way. They all do it.

"Hi." She stumbles over the single syllable word, and I stop myself from patting her head.

"You're very pretty." She's not, but I need the lies. They're more for her than for me. I know that at first she won't believe me, but if I suggest it, if I make her feel special, if I make her think she's worth *my* while, then god, those lies will pay up in spades.

Her eyes drop to her feet on cue, a dance I've done a hundred times before. I bring my knuckles to her chin and coax her head up waiting for her eyes to level with mine. "But you are."

Pink saturates her cheeks and those lips of hers pout and twist sending my cock into a frenzy. She doesn't answer; she cools off with her drink, trying to be nonchalant even when she's not. My mind reels with ideas for her.

"What's your name?"

"Eris." Her shy smile is more than adorable, it touches her lips, just a brief movement that's sexier and more seductive than it should be on a girl like her.

"That's a pretty name." I'll keep shovelling shit into her ears till she believes.

"Thanks." She shifts, her hands tangle together, dangling aimlessly in front of her.

"Are you here alone?"

"No." She shakes her head and her gaze drifts to the dance floor where three average-looking girls gyrate against one another. It's not sexy. Yet. But I know if I can get at least another one of them to join us I could make it work.

"Why aren't you dancing?" I lower my voice, her head drops just an inch, her chest expands with a sharp inhale. I bite down my smirk. It's pathetic how easy it all is.

She shrugs. "I don't really dance."

"That's a real shame. I bet you look sexy when you do." Lie number four; the more you stack up against one another, the bigger the reward.

The pink on her cheeks turns a dark red, and her eyes rake over her own pudgy body trapped in pink fabric that shows too many of her bulges and attributes. I won't be paying too much attention to those later. Her lips stretch into a sweet smile, her eyelids flutter one too many times.

"What's your name?" She changes tack on me.

"Michael." Of course, it's not, but who cares?

"Like the archangel?"

I smile, not just because she made the connection but because she is soon to learn I am more of a demon. Then again, the devil was an angel once. "One and the same. In fact, I was named after him."

"I can see why." She unnecessarily strokes my ego. I don't mind, as long as her tongue strokes my cock later on with as much enthusiasm.

I flash her the smile she's after and catch the way her eyes grow and her teeth bite into her lower lip. I've fucked around enough, time to test the water. I lean in close to her so that my breath tickles her skin and my husky whisper travels all the way inside her. "Tell me, Eris, do you know what girls without panties get?"

Her eyes turn into saucers, and she stares at my face, her mouth slightly open, just enough for me to stick a finger inside. I don't, but I could. She shakes her head, unable to speak. Just how I like it. Quiet and obedient.

"Drinks." I give her my answer and pull away, locking my eyes with hers. She steals another sharp breath, and her eyes flicker around the room like she's been caught doing something she shouldn't. Her meekness makes my cock hard as fuck. "Would you like a drink, Eris?"

She eyes her half-empty glass. I'm an optimist. I'm optimistic it's more empty than full and that she'd ask for a refill. In reality, it doesn't matter, when a guy like me offers a drink to a girl like her, they don't turn it down.

She nods and reaches for the glass slurping at the contents.

"Do you have panties on, Eris?"

"Yes," she stammers. Those lips of hers quiver, and every inch of me ignites.

"So what are we going to do about that?" I cock my head slightly and raise a single brow while maintaining a dashing smile I know gets her insides going.

She licks her lips as she thinks, and I clutch the chair I sit on, allowing her to tease me, without knowing. She'll pay for that later. Her eyes dart around till she spots the ladies room. My smile widens as I follow her gaze.

"I could go and take them off." Her voice is a choked broken whisper.

"I would like that very much." That's a lie, but I still wink at her and watch her whole body inhale.

The truth is I don't give a fuck if she keeps them on or not. At least with her underwear on, her oversized ass is contained. But the truth is she can't resist, not my charm, not my good looks, not my vicious invitations. She's drawn to me. It's not her fault, not really, but her eagerness to please me here and put herself in a precarious position for a mere alcoholic beverage, gives me hope for later tonight.

"Go on then." I wave her away. Her gaze flickers between the bathroom and me, and she reluctantly releases the glass she's still holding onto as if it's a lifebuoy and walks toward the bathroom.

I wave down a waiter and ask him to bring another of whatever she was drinking. It's not my job to know, or care. He comes back a few moments later and informs me it's a gin and tonic. Like I give a shit. My eyes are locked on the bathroom door, anticipation grips at my skin with tenter little hooks.

Eris walks out of the bathroom, and this time I can't help the smile that stretches itself across my face. I love when they do this for me. It makes them so uncomfortable. It's delightful to watch. Slow crafted steps. Fingers hovering at the hem of the dress, flushed hungry skin, large pupils and something part-guilt, part-lust freezing their face and forcing their eyes to flash across the room, worried that everyone knows. I feed on that insecurity. It means two things. One, she is eager and ready to do what I want. Two, she is uncomfortable enough to be willing to leave with me sooner rather than later.

She takes cautious steps back to the table, her eyes locked on mine, discomfort painted on her face like a Picasso.

"I got you a drink." I extend a hand and pull her to the table, holding her flush against me for a second, reminding her of her prize.

"Thank you." She reaches for it, but I grab her wrist, halting her progress.

"And what did you get for me?" I lean in and whisper into her ear. She swallows and glances up for a second before her eyes fall away. But not her hands, her hands rest on my hips, fingertips edging around, circling to my back. She wants to hold on.

"I've taken them off." Her voice rasps against my neck as she tiptoes, stretching herself against me.

She withdraws a little and opens her handbag and lets me peek at a pair of oversized, black lacy underwear.

"Mmmm," I murmur, "those could be anyone's."

Of course, I know they're hers, but what's the point of catching prey if you can't play with it a little? The best predators do; leopards, orcas, me.

I flash her more teeth and indicate that she should sit down. She does, her thighs firmly squeezed together. Her face the colour of ripe strawberries. I nudge her drink towards her and her fingers curl around the glass slicing through the condensation settled around it.

"Have a drink." The reward is for both of us. She gets to feel a little at ease and I get to watch her lips glisten with moisture as the alcohol makes them shimmer in the dim lights. She puts the glass down and waits. She knows what's coming.

"Let me see," I say and smile, waiting. Her eyes grow and thighs squeeze tighter, her chest rises and falls as she draws in desperate breaths. It's the smile that seals it usually. It makes my eyes twinkle and makes me seem more sincere, more believable. It's a fucking magic smile that leaves them mesmerised.

She's reluctant. I guess in some ways they all are, and still, she takes another sip, as if seeking courage in the form of alcohol. Her legs part slowly. She wills them to. An internal struggle rages inside her. I see it in the way her eyes dart around, in the way she licks her lips, and her hands are fisted so tightly on her tights they're bleached white. Still, she parts her legs for me, her dress inches upward, the flesh of her thighs eases away until at last, her pink pussy greets me.

"Oh so pretty," I rasp into her ear as she tries to clamp her legs shut. I step between her legs forcing them open around my broad shape "A very pretty pussy." I whisper in her ear and hear the harsh gasp. I smirk and drag my cheek along hers till my lips brush hers. Those thick parted lips that make me hard as a fucking rock. They shiver as I touch them, and the sensation ripples inside me.

Cockteaser.

I growl and snatch her lower lip between my teeth, dragging it slowly before I release her. Her heated eyes collide with mine till she rises and our mouths smash together. God, she's a good kisser which only makes me harder knowing she will probably suck me off just as well. I slip my hand between us and my finger slides along her wetness. She gasps and breaks away, but I bury my free hand in her hair and force her against me, forcing that hungry innocent mouth to meet mine. Fuck she tastes good, surprisingly so for a girl that looks like her.

Her body pulses. A thundering beat that my finger commands. I slip two fingers inside her and she sucks in a sharp breath leaving my mouth hollow. My thumb circles her clit, and she tries to pull away; she's worried people are watching. They probably are. Luckily I don't give a fuck, but she does, and I need her to, I need to push her just enough.

My fingers pump inside her, slow but harsh, my thumb circling, my mouth devouring hers. She moans into me, and the sound fills the dark void inside. It's delectable. Her hips begin to move, her eyes glaze, her hands exploring, fingers clawing, legs shaking and then I pull away.

She groans, disappointed, desperate.

Just the way I like them.

She's flushed, a sheen of sweat on her forehead, her chest an angry tide that rises and falls, her mouth glistens with my saliva, parted just enough for me to push my fingers inside. This time I do. Her eyes flicker open, growing large with the unexpected intrusion. I wait for a split-second before her mouth tightens, and I feel her suck down hard, cleaning my fingers, tasting herself, giving me a glimpse of what's to come.

I smirk. She's easy and willing, and goddam – that *mouth*. I pull my fingers out slowly till they pop, and her gaze drops away again. I coax her chin up. "Want to get out of here and have some fun?"

She nods. Of course she does. Her pussy must be throbbing, and her nipples are so hard they poke at the fabric of her dress. Her whole body sings with need, but then so does mine, and my needs always come first.

"Come on." I pull her off the chair and slip her hand into mine leading her away. It's part of the lie, the contact, she wants to believe it means more than it does. It makes her think she owns a part of me now.

She pulls and I stop, raising an eyebrow.

"I should tell my friends...."

"They'll be fine. And we're not going far." *Just to my apartment upstairs.*

If the way she sucked on my fingers is any indication, I'll be done quickly. Her friends won't even notice she's left, and maybe I can still get those two brunettes to come up later. I have plans for them. I smirk at the thought and yank her towards the back where my private elevator hides behind a locked door.

"Where are we going?" her voice trembles and I like that it does.

"To my apartment."

"You live here?"

"I do." I wink and watch her shiver. She's not cold, she just thinks she scored a really rich, incredibly good-looking guy. Which she hasn't. It's cute that she thinks girls like her get guys like me.

The elevator pings and I push her inside with my bigger body, pinning her to the wall, my hands on either side of her. Her breath falters as she looks up at me. I don't touch her, just keep her there, contained, barely breathing, needy and hungry. I need her hungry, starving, fucking famished. I need to feed her my cock.

Her eyes search mine. I wonder what she thinks she sees. Whatever it is, makes her tongue dart out and lick her lower lip. I groan and push my aching cock against her. Before she can reach for it the elevator door opens, but I don't step out, I don't let her move. I keep her there, locked, eager, waiting. And then at last she grips my cock.

The door closes again, and the elevator moves back downstairs. I let her touch me. Her fingers brush my shaft through the fabric. I don't move. Her eyes search mine for a second before undoing my belt and button; the slow nick of the zipper cuts through our breaths. I hiss as her fingers slip into my boxers and wrap around the shaft. I'm so hard it almost hurts.

Her fingers curl and squeeze, and my hips move on their own, the pressure too much, too little, not what I want. I freeze. "Not like this," I rasp.

The door to the elevator pings open again, only a locked white door behind us and the thumping of the music that seeps from beneath.

Her teeth bite into the red plump flesh of her lower lip and her hands pull my cock out of its fabric cage. It jerks in the colder air, but I know it's about to get real hot.

Eris falls to her knees before me, just as a worshipper does before her god. Her long eyelashes flutter and a droplet of pre-cum glistens on my cock. Her swift tongue sweeps it away, and I groan at the sensation. The door shuts behind us and we start moving again as she wraps her delectable fucking lips around my shaft at last.

I growl, she's just the right combination of soft and hard. Her hands work my balls as her hot mouth plays havoc on my sanity. My hands fist her hair, nails digging into her scalp. She moans and flounders at my forcefulness, but I don't let up. I guide her mouth as I expand inside her.

Sweat breaks on my forehead as pleasure builds up inside me, release calling my name from a distance. My jaw clenches, my whole body tight as I pump my hips, fucking her mouth. I think she's gagging, but it doesn't matter, not when I'm this close. My head rears back as my cock hits the back of her throat. With the mirrors above me, I see her trying to fight me off, fighting for air, I see her swallowing what I give her.

My breaths become shallow, streaming out of me in harsh pants. I am on the precipice. Devine pleasure only a few more mouthfuls away. Tightness grips my spine and rolls into my balls. My back bows, my abs clench, my knees want to buckle, and then my body freezes, gripped by a stone-like stillness as I come hard and fast. My cock jerks inside her mouth and spurts hot cum into the back of her throat, pulsing inside.

My head hangs as if my neck is too tired to hold it up. My body comes back down to earth as the doors ping again. Eris wipes her mouth, her sweaty flushed face is tear streaked.

"Fuck," is all I say as I step back and lean against the elevator wall. I think we're moving again.

She nears me. I think she wants a kiss, but she is fucking dreaming if she thinks I'm going to touch her mouth again after I've emptied myself inside it. I halt her progress by tucking myself back in, and she tilts her head as if she doesn't understand.

"Are we going to your apartment now?" she asks and despite the fact she just swallowed my dick like a pro she sounds so timid, I almost feel sorry for her. But not really.

"What for?"

She chews on her lower lip for a second and her hands lace together. "You said we were going to have fun."

She sounds desperate and clingy and oh so uncertain. It's pathetic. "I did, thanks."

"But—"

"Look," the elevator door opens again, then shuts behind us, "you wanted to have fun. I let you suck my cock. Not sure what else you want, but someone like me doesn't end up with someone like you. So go finish that drink I bought you and watch your friends dance, and maybe later I'll take one of them upstairs and actually make it to my bed."

Her breath heaves in and out as I speak. Her already flushed face turns a dark angry red matching her flaring messed-up hair that stands in unnatural waves. I guess I can understand her frustration. After all, I did lie to her, and it's not like I'm going to make her come; she can do that work herself.

"Liar," she seethes.

"I didn't lie, sweetheart." *I did.* "You made assumptions."

"I...I...you..." she stutters, and I bark out a harsh laugh.

"There's no you and I. I just let you suck me off, and you got your pretty little pussy touched a little. Not sure why you're still complaining."

At my words her face twists. And it's not just her lips or her eyes or her forehead, it's as if the skin has turned liquid and detaches itself from the skull. Her entire face convulses. I take a backwards step and my back hits the wall. Her body shakes, and I rub my eyes in disbelief as I watch her limbs elongate and thin out, her long red hair turns a shade of sky blue; her shallow eyes narrow into piercing brown saucers with golden flakes.

I stand. Frozen. My mind unable to comprehend what it thinks it sees. But the tubby redhead who had me in her mouth moments ago has vanished, and in her place stands the most beautiful woman I have ever seen. A woman whose looks I could compare to my own. Flawless, god-like, perfect.

Her tight body is squeezed into a little black dress, and long black boots slither just below her knees. The blue hair cascades in gentle waves over her shoulders and the gold shimmers in her eyes as she glares at me.

"What the f—"

"You dare lie to me?"

"What the hell is going on?"

She rushes over. A lightning bolt of movement, nothing but a flash – stunning and unnatural all at once. Her fingers wring around my neck, and I'm suspended in her grasp as if I am nothing but a sack of feathers.

She starts to speak. But whatever she says makes no sense. The words do not exist. Not in any language I know, yet they are as enchanting as she is. I watch her lips move, but the words turn to noise. An angry hum swirls around me. The first sting pierces my neck, then another in my lower back and a third on the back of my hand. I scream, but there's no sound, just the angry swarm, as if she's unleashed a hive of fiery hornets inside my body and they sting me mercilessly.

My body burns, my vision blurs, and the last thing I remember is a blue-haired beauty standing over my broken body.

2

DORIAN

"The worst thing about being lied to is knowing you weren't worth the truth." — Jean-Paul Sartre

My head hurts.

I scuttle against the wall. Shards of broken mirror lay scattered across the floor like snow. They nick at my hands and legs. I pull them away as I sit up. My head whips right and left, but I'm alone. The elevator door opens again and I'm back on the first floor. I stand, brushing myself off. A few strands of hair decorate my shoulder.

Did that actually just happen?

I rake a hand through my hair. A number of strands come away in my palm and I make a note to run my comb through it again later. I shrug, then straighten my shirt and make my way back to the bar where I sit and signal to the barman to get me a drink. He stares at me for a few seconds too long before placing my tumbler of Dalmore whiskey in front of me, and I take a long hard sip as I sweep the bar searching for Eris. No sign of her at all. I do notice her three friends; they are still dancing, gyrating against each other on the dance floor, touching and caressing one another in ways designed to grab attention.

And now they have mine.

I picture them naked on my bed, three pairs of tits, three tongues. Oh so many hot wet holes. I drain my glass, abandoning it on the bar and make my way to the three women whose bodies are like a wave of seduction designed to drench men and leave them wasted.

I approach, casual, aloof, certain in the way I always am. I know that I won't have to work hard to persuade them to come upstairs and give me my own personal show. My face will do most of the work for me.

"Hello, ladies." I use my friendliest huskiest voice. "I'm a friend of Eris."

They stop, look at me then grimace. *They actually fucking grimace.* At me? I look behind me, wondering. "We don't know anyone named Eris, and what's wrong with your face?"

The one who speaks cringes then grabs her friends and they step away from me, deeper into the dance floor and the arms of other predators.

What the fuck just happened?

My hand shoots to my face, but I can't feel anything. What is she on about? I rush to the bathroom, shove the door open and make a beeline for the mirror. I stall. My heart stammers in my chest as I look at myself. I stare. My eyes grow as disbelief sinks down into my belly. My perfect complexion is marred with tiny angry red veins that entwine like streams across my face. As if my skin thinned out and my muscles vanished and all that's left is angry blood vessels that pop below.

I poke the skin, unsure what I'm trying to achieve;

whether I'm still trying to believe this is my face or if I hope to push back the angry bloody rivulets. The vein in my neck ticks.

What the fuck is going on?

Cold water cascades down my face as I run it under the tap. It does nothing to settle the redness. If anything, I can feel the arteries throb as they flow inside me with each of my heartbeats.

"Fuck this," I say to no one and storm from the bathroom and to my elevator.

||||

I stomp around my apartment like a caged animal. My face set in a scowl, my muscles ache and shiver under all my anger. I suck in a few calming breaths and return to the mirror. This time she is kinder. The red blemishes dim and fade as if I'd imagined the whole thing. I shake my head wanting to dislodge the feelings rising up inside me. Maybe a quick fuck will help me get rid of this budding anxiety. My face isn't quite perfect yet, and so trying to pick up downstairs again seems like a waste of time. I can call one of my usuals and keep the light off. I reach for my phone and scroll.

Cassandra. Sweet little Cassandra. That woman is more desperate than a starving kid. She will do just about anything I ask as long as I give her some attention. Stringing her along has become not only an art form but a source of entertainment. I'm going to see how far I can push her, how many lies I can make her swallow before she realises there never was and never will be a future for us.

"Hello?" Her sleepy voice rings through the phone.

"It's me."

"Oh hi." She perks up.

"I've missed you," I say. *I haven't.*

As the words leave my mouth noise fills my head. It takes me a few seconds to realise I'm the one who's screaming.

The phone falls from my hand as pain erupts across my face. A sickening snapping sound echoes in my ear and blood gushes from my nose. The hot liquid running through my hands and flooding my mouth, soaking my tongue and my clothes.

The pain jolts throughout my body and every muscle feels weak, loses tension, my knees wobble like my bones have all melted. I drop down, gurgling on the floor like a helpless fucking animal. I think I can hear Cassandra screaming my name. My body burns, my vision blurs, and the last thing I remember is pain.

||||

When I wake up, I am in my bed. Although I distinctly remember passing out on the floor. I look around my room. Nothing seems disturbed or out of the ordinary except for the fact I'm naked under the sheets; my hard morning erection grapples with the sheet.

A finger of light creeps from behind the curtain and onto the wall. I look at my watch; it's after ten in the morning. My gaze sweeps the floor; my clothes aren't here. My hand shoots to my face. I trace my nose, and that's when I feel it. I shoot from the bed, a rain of hair lands on my shoulders. I brush it away and run to my mirror. I stare at my face. My perfect, flawless, beautiful face, and that's when

I see it. There's a kink on the bridge of my nose, a slight protrusion, minute really. Almost undetectable.

Almost.

My fingers feather the skin, then push and prod. The bone is set and there's no pain. Just imperfection. I glare at my face; it's like looking at a stranger. This small change feels unsurmountable. A blemish on what otherwise would be perfection.

I run my finger against the kink, willing it to vanish. But all it does is glare back at me, mocking. I draw in a long breath and step back, tilting my head from one side to the other, then smile at the fresh scar. Interesting people have scars; soldiers, warriors, people who have truly lived. They have stories, and I am a man full of stories, and when they ask me... I will turn this scar into my most beautiful lie.

3

AFTER

JINX

"All truth is simple... is that not doubly a lie?" – Fredrich Nietzsche

Rain batters my windscreen, and the wind shakes the trees as I drive along the too long driveway and pull up to the estate. Killing the engine, I stare at the house that has no business looking like it does on the edge of suburbia. A white double storey structure, sun-bleached and weather-beaten. Black shutters hang across the windows shutting out the sun. Maybe at one time it was grand, but now it sits derelict and uncared for; the only sign of wealth is the large plot of land it sits on and the strangely manicured garden surrounding it.

I sigh, getting out and opening the boot. Pulling out my cleaning supplies, the frigid wind washes over me, stealing the little warmth I have left. When Amanda told me about this job, I jumped at it. Five hundred dollars a week cleaning a house. Of course I took it. Looking at it now, I probably should have asked more questions; like why no one else wanted the job and why so many other girls started and never finished the contract.

Whatever. Easy money, just clean up some rich guy's house. Amanda did say he was a little odd; a recluse who shut himself off from the world. Apparently, once upon a time, he was some hotshot. I shrug at the thought. I guess sometimes we all need a little bit of space. There have been rumours of ghosts on the property for years, but I keep telling myself those are just silly stories made up by bored rich people as I make my way along the path towards the house.

I trudge up to the front of the house, rain smashing against my body, plastering my hair to my face. At the court-yard, the ground is paved. A stunning delicate mosaic lays at my feet; the face of a beautiful angelic woman with flowing blue hair and piercing brown eyes with golden flakes. It looks almost life-like, and a shiver runs through me as the eyes bore into mine. I tip-toe around the image, my skin crawling with uneasiness.

The path to the door is lined with bushes of red roses. Even for this time of year they are perfect, each one plump and deep red. The place feels off. Out of place. An uneasy feeling crawls along my skin like bugs wriggling just beneath the surface. I shake it off and knock on the large wooden door, but no one answers. I was told no one would, but it feels unnatural to walk uninvited into a stranger's house. Of course, it's not the first time a client hasn't been home when I've arrived, but I like to make my presence known; somehow it feels less intrusive.

Another gust of wind has me hissing for breath, the cold penetrating my thin black jumper as if I was standing completely naked. Whatever heat remains beneath my skin is leaching out fast. I count to ten, then knock again. When still no one answers after my third knock, I slide the heavy silver key into the door and push it open. It moans like a sick woman, and a shiver runs along my spine.

I shake it off and move into the house. "Hello?"

I stand frozen in the grand entryway that has no business being inside a weathered estate. My voice reverberates in the empty space and I'm greeted with a long hard silence. The wind lashes my freezing body, snatching away my hellos.

"Anyone here?" I call out.

I take a ginger step inside, hefting my heavy equipment and pushing my backpack onto my shoulders. Heat brushes my face and, without thinking, I take another step inside and seal the door behind me.

My eyes sweep the space. I feel like I have walked out of reality and into a fairy tale. The house is totally at odds with itself. While the outside gives the impression of a rundown deserted estate house, the interior could have at one time been an exquisite mansion. I can tell even from where I stand that everything is still in pristine condition, it just needs a little bit of love. And when I say a little bit, I mean a shit tonne. I let out a long sigh. Fuck Amanda.

I drop my bucket full of cleaning bottles and rags and the vacuum in my other hand and take another step inside. I run my hand over a wooden shelf tucked along the thick stone wall. It leaves a long dark groove in the deep layer of dust. My fingertip is grey and grimy, and I rub the dirt on the back of my jeans.

"Anyone here?" I call out as heat bites my cold skin and seeps inside. The looming entrance is mostly bare, an unused coat hanger, a lone empty shelf that runs the length of the wall and an unnecessarily tall ceiling that makes the space feel like a cavern.

I walk deeper into the house, my eyes catching the flickering from the next room. A roaring fire heats the large room to my right, and I step inside. The room is scantily furnished, a high-backed chair stands alone in the centre with a footstool before it. A small table stands near it, a stack of books piled on top. These are the only three items not entirely covered in dust. The hearth, glass bookshelf and grandfather clock all wear a layer of dust like a thick cloak.

I stretch my hands over the fire, the heat bleeding into me, stinging my skin, when a clatter startles me and I spin towards the noise.

"You're late." The voice is raspy and angry and doesn't sound altogether human. I swivel and search the room. Emptiness stares back at me.

"Hello?"

"You're late," the voice repeats, fiercer this time.

I start to back away, my eyes sweeping the room, searching the few darkened corners. "Yes, I know, it's just that I had class and the weather changed and—"

"You were meant to be here hours ago." He feels somehow closer yet the more I look the less I see, it's like being haunted by a shadow.

I inch backwards towards the hallway. "Look, I'm sorry, I'm here now, I can just get starte—"

"Leave now and come back on time tomorrow!"

"I... But..."

"I. Said. Leave!" The angry growl booms in the room, echoing off the walls.

I run out of the hallway and through the front door which sways behind me as I rush along the paved path and down towards my car. The cold takes my breath away, the wind smashing against my skin. The cold, harsh, sky is greyish and menacing and yet I felt more threatened when I was inside with the fire and the heat.

My teeth chatter as I slam the car door behind me and start my engine, putting my foot down and swerving out of the driveway and back to the city. Fuck this. I'll find another way to pay my bills.

4

DORIAN

**"Lying is done with words and also with silence" –
Adrienne Rich**

Moving to the window, I watch as the intruder runs towards her car. My skin itches. Why is she here now? She almost caught me, in my own fucking house. I'll have to have words with Amanda about making sure her girls arrive on time. Providing she manages to find a new one to send over.

She's tiny, her jacket barely covering her petite figure. Her raven black hair billows in the harsh wind and she reminds me of a wet cat; pathetic and miserable. I grit my teeth thinking of how easily I would have taken her *before*. The thought is like sand in my mouth, and I swallow it down. My body shivers, remembering what it was like to touch another person. A *woman*. Their soft delectable skin and hot mouths. Something akin to desire stirs inside me, but nothing else happens. My broken body doesn't react at all. I growl and step away from the window as she slams the door to her car and speeds away.

I move out of the shadows where I'm now forced to live my life. In darkness, in hiding. My head itches. I pick at the dry skin; one of many bald patches that have carved themselves into my scalp. I flick away dead scabs and walk towards the hallway where I find her discarded items. I examine them.

A bucket, a bunch of cheap cleaning solutions in a variety of spray bottles, some rags, and a vacuum cleaner that will probably need to be recharged by morning. I shake my head at the pathetic scene, when something else catches my eye.

The backpack is what artists and poets would call well worn, but really, it's an old piece of shit that should have been thrown out years ago, but for some unknown reason, she's decided to hold on to this barely-held-together crap heap and keep it alive. I shake my head and reach for it. It's heavier than I thought it would be. Dragging it behind me and into the lounge room, I make my way to my winged armchair and let the fire warm my skin. The heat makes it itch more. I ignore it.

I treat the bag like an antique, not because it's special, but because I can't fathom the thought of having to clean up one more mess when this tattered fabric comes apart in my hands.

I remember reading an article in a glossy magazine once, something about what the contents of a handbag say about the girl. I thought it could be helpful to separate the crazy ones from the girls who understand they are nothing but a hole. That article was fucking useless; the only thing I learned about women's handbags is that all women carry shit around and none of it means anything.

I reach inside the smaller pocket in the front. There is

nothing useful there; a few pens, a pack of gum, a bunch of hair ties and a few loose coins. I fish around for a loose stick of lipstick or some eyeshadow. She carries none. It's odd that a girl like her isn't trying to enhance her features with some makeup, given her plain looks. I close the zip again and have a sudden need to wipe my hand on something. I reach into the main pocket and pull out three books.

She carries a copy of *A Tale of Two Cities*, a classic. Post-it notes poke out from every page covered in scribbles. There's a textbook about the fundamentals of writing, and the last is a book about myths and legends across the century. I frown as I set them aside.

She's doing a literature course at the local university. How poignant. Still, she's cleaning toilets for a living, so either she's a starving artist or just not that intelligent. It's probably the latter. Still, this backpack has told me very little about her. Till I retrieve the last item in the bag. A stack of papers all handwritten. The ink is smudged in places and the writing is rushed, the corners of the pages tattered and folded as if she's been carrying them for a long time. At last, something with a personality.

I look at the first page. "*Fairytales and other truths*" is the title which, despite myself, instantly has me interested. I leaf through the pages and read over the first few lines, the story is about a beast and a curse. I grind my teeth and collect my thoughts for a few moments.

I pull out my phone, my fingers fluttering over the papers. Amanda answers on the second ring.

"Hello?"

I hate the way she tries to sweeten her voice every time we speak. Ever since she realised I had money, she's spoken to me differently. She reeks of greed and worthlessness, and if I could have it my way, I'd discard her like the piece of trash she is.

"It's me."

"What can I do for you, Mr. Stone?"

"The girl you sent today was late."

"Apologies, she was told—"

"That's not really good enough, is it?" *She almost fucking caught me.*

"I'm sorry, I'll—"

"You'll what? None of the girls you've sent over have been of much use."

There's a short silence. I hear her draw a breath and I know she's preparing herself. She's not the first to try and do this. "I am trying to find someone to suit your needs, but you must understand—"

"No, *you* must understand, I have been paying you a nice little retainer just to stay on your books and so far, all I've gotten was a collection of useless girls who do a half-assed job at the best of times, and never finish. And now, not only did this one run out of here, she left all her '*stuff*'." I wave my hand at the collection I've pulled out of her backpack. "In my hallway."

"I'm sorry, I'll ha—"

"Yes, have her pick it up, and she better be here at the right fucking time." I end the call and set the phone down, running my hands over the stacks of paper. They seem important, but they can wait. I was in the middle of something.

5

JINX

**"That was how dishonesty and betrayal started, not in big
lies but in small secrets" – Amy Tan**

The rhythmic cadence of the train turns into a
harsh squeal before the horn blares through the
window overhanging my bed and drags me from
sleep. Or maybe it's the fact that my teeth are chattering.

Fuck. I'll have to pay that gas bill eventually.

Curled up under my thin blanket I breathe hot air onto
my knees, my skin burning at the warmth, seeking more.
The chill has cemented itself under my skin and keeps me
rooted in place. Just a few more months of this and then I
will get my Bachelor of Arts degree.

It's laughable. Everyone told me an arts degree will get
me nowhere, but I wanted to prove them wrong. The university promised internships and industry connections, neither
of which is really true, so here I am six months from graduating, with two potential prospects but almost zero money
in my bank account.

I inhale and watch the air turn to vapour in front of my face as I exhale harshly thinking about yesterday. That job, that man. No, he wasn't a man, he was a creep, my skin crawls with the memory, and I shudder.

My alarm goes off and I reach over, silencing it. I need to get up, I have class in an hour. Sitting up, a sudden sickening feeling overwhelms me. I bolt out of my bed. Flooded with adrenaline, I begin a frantic search of my apartment, looking for my backpack.

"No, no, no, no, no." I shake my head violently as the adrenaline begins to dissolve, and my backpack is nowhere to be seen. Grabbing a hoodie, I pull it on and snatch my keys, rushing to my car. My toes sting as they hit cold concrete, and my heart thunders inside me as the grey sky threatens to open up.

I tear my car apart searching beneath the seats and in the empty boot, already knowing what I am looking for isn't there. A dozen needles dance their way across my forehead as I keep searching, my breath coming in short, sharp pants, and my clammy hands grabbing at empty space.

"No, no, no, fuck," I fall into the passenger seat drawing in breath, my head falling into my palms. *My backpack. Fuck.* Tears burn my eyes as fear threatens to swallow me whole. My dissertation is in there. I mean sure, it doesn't look like much now, just scribbled stories on a stack of paper, but I was going to type it all out this weekend and hand it in early. I've been working on that book for a fucking year. Hours of writing and collecting just the perfect words, sewing them together seamlessly, and now, I've left it at that freak's house.

I suck in a few breaths trying to collect my frazzled thoughts. It's fine, I can just go over there and ask for my things back. They are mine, it will be fine. I keep breathing, calming my thrashing heart and sucking air into my lungs. I'll just go over there, everything will be fine.

6

DORIAN

"Lies are the greatest murderers. They kill the truth" – Socrates

There's an unexpected knock on the door. Whoever it is, is unwelcome. I ignore it but it continues, the banging drilling a hole into my brain.

I leave what I am doing and rush to the door only to find the black-haired girl from yesterday shivering on the other side. She's here at the wrong time.

Again.

I clench my jaw, even as a strange foreign feeling glides inside me. Clearly, Amanda needs to be spoken to... again. I may have to get Victor involved. I wipe my hands on my pants and unlatch the door then scuttle into the shadows.

"Come."

The door inches open and the woman steps inside, hesitant. She looks around, suspicious, scared, apprehensive. She sweeps the room, looking into the shadows, searching, looking. For me.

"Hello?"

I say nothing, just watch her. Her gaze travels the length of the hallway floor, and I realise what she is actually looking for. A slow smile creeps along my face.

When she finds nothing, she makes her way back to my lounge room where the fire is roaring. She stands with her back to the flames, her gaze darting around the room taking everything in. My chair, the footrest, and the empty shelves and walls. There is nothing for her to see here, anything that means anything to me has been locked away years ago, and the rest has long since turned to dust.

"Hello?"

"You are too early," I say from my hiding place and watch her jump out of her skin. Her body stiffens into a battle-ready stance. Interesting. I feel like I should apologise for scaring her, but I'm not sorry. The way she recoiled made her pretty little tits jump. And I don't want to lie. I can't. I grit my teeth as a shadow of Eris crosses my mind. The thought makes my scalp itch again. I ignore it.

"Where are you?" Her eyes flicker around the room.

I ignore her question and repeat myself, "You're too early."

"Too early for what?" Her wary tone travels up to me as she keeps searching the shadows.

"For cleaning."

"I'm not here for that."

"Oh?" It's been a while since I've played games... well... with anyone, and she seems like such a lovely mouse to throw around.

"I... erm... yesterday I forgot my things here..."

"Forgot?"

She clears her throat. "Left them behind." She sounds apologetic, it's sweet, but wasted.

I remain hidden and watch the trespasser. She nears my

chair again; long fingers trail the exquisitely carved wood and plush fur trim. I wonder if her pedestrian little brain can see the minute modifications I've had to make to accommodate for my new shape.

When I remain silent, she carries on. "I need my things back."

"In time."

She shuffles around, her eyes always searching.

"I don't have time. I need to get to class."

Ah yes. "You can come back after class then."

"No, I need my things back now."

"What's your name?" I ignore her question.

She sighs. "Jade Hix, but everyone calls me Jinx."

"Jinx?" A cold piercing shiver crawls up my spine. "Are you a bearer of bad luck?" She shrugs. Maybe she realises how ridiculous it sounds. Well, a stupid name for a stupid girl. At least the only person I can still lie to is myself and I pretend not to feel the shiver that slithers down my spine. Is she another curse?

"Look, can I get my things back now? I really have to get going." She's talking and stalking at the same time, creeping little steps inching forwards, searching.

"I will set your cleaning things in the hall for collection after your school day, I will leave the door unlocked."

She clears her throat. "My backpack? I need it..."

"You can have that too."

The tension in her face falls away. "That's great, but can I get that all now? I don't want to be late to class."

"Oh? But you have no issues coming *here* at all the wrong times."

She huffs. "I'm sorry about that. My things?"

"Can be collected later."

"Why?"

I grind my teeth, the uneven fangs moving in my gums. I

taste blood. "Cause I'm not ready, I wasn't expecting... Company..."

Her eyes narrow as she tries to find me in dark corners. There is not much for her to see; I keep everything hidden away. "Show yourself."

"I think I have been more than patient."

"But my things—"

"Will be returned later," I growl, and she shivers. I don't think it's from the cold.

"Later?"

"Yes. This afternoon."

"This afternoon?"

"Yes." The word comes out on a sigh. It's like talking to an echo with this girl, repeating everything I say.

She nods. Thank fuck she understands something.

||||

The knock comes just on time, and I am fucking giddy. It's been so long since I've had any fun, and it's about to begin. This day that started out just as another mundane waste of time has suddenly turned into something full of potential.

"Come," I say, hiding in the shadows, swallowing down my barely contained excitement as Jinx walks in, the gaping front door swallowing her like a beast.

"Hello?" Her eyes sweep the hallway floor where I have placed her things. Her gaze lands on the backpack and she lunges for it, snatching it into her arms and ripping open the zip. She pulls out the three books and empties the contents just to find that what she's really after is gone.

"Where's my book?" Her cream complexion pales.

"Right there next to you," I smirk to myself.

"Not these... the other one... the hand writ... you, you went through my things?"

"*My* things. You left them here and they automatically became mine." I delight in the horror etched on her face, as vivid as a painting, frozen in a moment of fear. I think of at least one wall I would hang it on, and my smile widens.

"What? That's not how it works. Where the hell is my thesis?" Her head flings from side to side as she examines every dark space in the room.

"It's very well written. Well, the parts that aren't complete garbage."

Her mouth falls open for just a second, and her eyes narrow. "You read it?"

"Of course." She asks a lot of stupid questions.

"You shouldn't have done that. It's not yours. Now give it back, I need to hand it in." Red leaks into her cheeks and her eyes are wide saucers. She's a little rabbit in a very large trap and she is slowly beginning to realise it.

"I don't think you get to tell me what to do in my own house." I don't mean to retort as loudly as I do. Her head jerks up and she takes a few backwards steps, her eyes darting from side to side. *Fuck.*

She draws in a few sharp breaths looking like she might pass out. I hope she doesn't. Deadweight is an annoying thing to move around. I wait for her to settle a little.

"I... I just need it, please. Give it back and you'll never see me again."

I tilt my head at my little mouse. Doesn't she realise that's exactly what I want? "I plan to."

She remains silent, waiting, and I let her wait, stretching out her panic like a bowstring, till the tension filling the room is just right to unleash my words.

"I will return one page for each day you come and clean my house."

"What? No, that's blackmail." She trembles, her face twisted like a gnarled tree in a haunted forest.

"Is it?"

"Yes! Give me back my work."

"You will get it back if you do what you're told."

"You can't do this!"

"Okay. You can let yourself out."

"Wait..."

I do. In silence.

"I need it back," she whines.

"I've explained my terms, Jinx. Take it or leave it."

Her gaze searches the room, wandering along the walls and shadowy spaces. "Fuck this!" she yells at the air. Of course, she's aiming her words at me, but she misses. Tears pool in her eyes and I can't quite tell if she's angry or petrified. Not that it really matters.

She snatches the items I've left on the floor and storms out of the house. This is going to be fun.

7

JINX

"Man is least himself when he talks in his own person. Give him a mask and he will tell you the truth." – Oscar Wilde

The audacity! Who does that asshole think he is? Taking my things, rifling through my bag, *reading* my work, invading my privacy! I shove the cleaning stuff into the boot, throwing it violently. And then he wants to blackmail me for my own work? I throw the bucket into the boot and it clatters in the back, all the bottles falling out like confetti. I swipe away my unshed tears.

Fuck him and fuck this. I can just rewrite it all, it's all mostly in my head, right?

I slam my boot shut and hightail it to class, not that it matters, I'll be late anyway.

||||

Professor Burns made sure to humiliate me as I tried to sneak into his class. That arrogant fuck thinks he's better than all of us cause he can recite the classics. Once, he told me it's a motivational tool; pulling us down so we can crawl our way up and prove him wrong. I think he's just a bully and we're perfect targets. Helpless and totally at his mercy. I've been feeling that a lot lately.

The couch is worn out and musty, its faded upholstery showing signs of wear and tear. It sits slightly askew, the once plush cushions sagging under the weight of forgotten memories. I've thought about getting rid of it for ages, but something about it appeals to me. We're both a little faded, a little broken, but there is still life inside us. My laptop sits across my lap, and I stare at the little black line as it flickers at me in anticipation. The words hang on my tongue, wanting to be written, and yet every time I start, the words feel wrong and I delete my efforts. It's like my brain is locked up and my work refuses to come out of its newfound vault.

"Fuck this." I get up and tear my hands through my hair, this is bullshit. I can do this, it's easy. I've done it before.

I ditch the laptop and take the steps to the small kitchen. My old refrigerator hums in the corner, drowned out by the occasional thundering of trains as they pass overhead. The stovetop and sink bear the remnants of hastily prepared meals, remnants of a life lived in perpetual haste.

The tap groans as I fill my glass and gulp the water hoping to cleanse my burning insides, settle the angry anxiety and find words through the chaos that churns inside me.

I grab my writing pad and pen. I've always been more comfortable on paper. There's a sense of freedom there, an ability to just spew out words without the constant need to self-edit. Crawling onto my bed, the sunken mattress dips further under my weight as I tuck my feet beneath the dishevelled pile of sheets on the other end. Resting the pad on my knees, I tap the paper. Words slither beneath my skin, begging for an escape route just to be trapped inside my head.

"Fuck!" I throw the pad away and stare at the sky through the small window above my bed. The air is heavy, the humidity presses down on me, suffocating. Black clouds sprawl across the sky draining whatever light was cast by the moon, leaving the world a place of dark shadows. I slam my head into my pillow. I'll try again tomorrow.

||||

Three days of emptiness follow me around like a shadow. No matter how hard I try, the words remain locked inside me. Or maybe it's just the opposite. I've already set them free once and they refuse to return to their cage.

The reality is, as much as I try, I can't seem to duplicate what I already have, and I just don't have enough time to fashion a whole new manuscript to the level I had finally gotten my final draft. It's been months of writing, research, hours spent in libraries buried in books, forfeiting meals for time on computers, and late nights scribbling thoughts in a deranged sleepless frenzy.

I need my thesis desperately. It is my way out. This work is the escape I've been desperate for, the open door that will let me finally get away and live the life *I* want. Away from *him* and his lies, away from this squalor I have run to. I already have two offers for publication...

I surrender to the inevitable.

P ulling up to the estate, I glare at the house. The greying white colour that peels away at the edges of the weatherboards, the moss-covered roof and the gaping door that looms over the entrance.

It's 3.55 p.m. My head sinks into my palms and I rub my eyes. What the fuck am I doing?

Sliding out of my car, I take a steeling breath and move to the door, knocking.

"Come."

I push the door open, finding it unlocked. Stepping inside, trepidation drips inside me like poison. "Hello?"

"You're on time. Good." His patronising tone slinks beneath my skin, agitating me. *Asshole.*

"I need my paper back."

"Do we have a deal?" He cuts straight to the chase.

"How do I know you'll keep your end of the bargain?"

"I have no need for your work."

"So why keep holding on to it?'

"Because I have *other* needs." All the hair on my body stands at attention and my skin blooms with goosebumps.

"Cleaning needs?"

"You can start now." He doesn't affirm my question. "You can work for two hours and then I will return one page."

"I didn't bring my things."

"I've left everything you might need in the lounge. You can start there. I'll come find you when you're done."

I wait for more, but all that follows is silence. Huffing out an annoyed breath, I step into the lounge where the fire is still burning and find a collection of rags, cleaning products and dusters.

I move around the lounge area. It feels unlived in, just

decorative despite its obvious functionality. The strange, deformed armchair rests in front of the fire with a smaller footstool. A fire roars in the stone hearth giving the room an orange glow. There is not much more; no trinkets or paintings, no sign of a life lived. The owner keeps his life as hidden as he does himself. Large heavy curtains shield the windows, darkening the room. I bet that if I open them, grey light would flood the room and give it some life. I don't, not today.

I look around the dusty room, sigh, then get to work.

8

DORIAN

"And after all, what is a lie? Tis but the truth in masquerade" – Lord Byron

I watch her clean. It's mesmerising, the way her body moves in space. Perhaps it's been too long since I've had someone in my space, or maybe it's because she is different than the other girls. Her body is here, her limbs move – meticulously. She does her job well, but her mind is elsewhere. I can see her sunk in a myriad of thoughts. She's not so much drowning as is being consumed by them. She's a fascinating creature. I think I'll enjoy dissecting her.

The clock ticks the time away, an hour then two. I wonder if she notices I let her continue past her due time. It's not a test or a punishment, more like tax for time owed. She has interrupted my other activities. Twice.

I let another thirty minutes go by before I scurry downstairs and back into the shadows of the room. "Your work time is done."

Her body jerks and stiffens, and I delight in the reaction.

She is such a lovely little mouse. She collects herself quickly and puts the rags down, she does so with great care and I'm unsure if she's trying to be careful or silent.

"Great, I'd like my page now."

"Indeed." She did a fine job, the woodwork that has for so long been dull with a layer of dust now gleams with polish, and the room looks like it has taken a deep breath in, feeling almost larger. Or maybe it's her presence. Suddenly I do not want my little mouse to scurry away so soon. Despite my reluctance, I pull out the first page I have tucked in my hand. "Turn around."

She scans the room, searching. "Why?"

"Do you want your page or not?"

She huffs out a little sound but does as she's told. A satisfied smirk crosses my lips. Walking into the room, I brush by her, close enough to get a little whiff of her fruity scent and watch her shiver as she feels my cloak kiss her skin. I set the page on my chair and retreat into the shadows.

"You may turn back now," I say and watch as she whirls around in a flurry, her gaze sweeping the room, hoping.

When she can't find me, she walks to the chair and snatches the paper I've set there for her. "What the fuck is this?"

"The first page, as agreed."

"It's only the title page."

Glee fills me like a dam. "It is."

"What the fuck am I meant to do with it?"

"I've kept my part of the bargain."

She grinds her teeth, irritation seeping off her quivering body. "This is bullshit!" she yells at the room, and my heart rate spikes for the first time in I don't know how long.

Interesting.

"You can come back tomorrow to earn another page." I let her sit with that for a second. "Or..."

Her eyes lift from the page in her hand. "Or?"

I finger the yellowing paper with its tattered edges in my hand, "How would you like to earn a second page?"

I watch as her teeth chew on her bottom lip and her eyes widen a fraction as she lets my words stick like Velcro to her tiny brain. "What would I have to do?" Her voice is hoarse as her eyes drop back to the paper in her hand.

I fight back the chuckle that builds inside me, I can see the path her little mind takes her down, but what's even more amusing is that she is earnestly considering doing whatever I ask. Good, this might be easier than I thought. "I want you to pull down your jeans all the way to your ankles then bend over my chair. Keep your eyes down till I tell you otherwise."

She gapes before she stammers, "I... I don't understand..."

"There's nothing to understand." Her body tenses as I continue. "Do you want your second page or not?"

Her jaw clenches, tiny muscles dancing around before she takes a few heavy-footed strides towards my chair. She stands there, hovering, waiting for more. She is rather slow.

"I will give you your page now, and you will read it to me."

"What? No!" Her voice carries over to me.

"If you prefer, I can feed it to this fire."

"No! Don't." Defeat stains her voice and joy swells inside me like a tide. "Okay, I'll do it."

"Go on then. Jeans down, bend over and get your face close enough to the page so you can read it to me."

She stands there still as a corpse for a few more seconds before slowly undoing the button to her jeans. She clutches onto the fabric for a few seconds as if it is some kind of life-line, before finally pulling them all the way down, revealing her shapely legs and black cotton underwear. Then she hesitantly bends over, her hands crawling over the thick leather of the chair and gripping the sides, her knuckles blanching.

"Don't turn around," I warn her, and she shivers under my threat. Her head moves an inch, a tiny barely noticeable nod of understanding.

I position myself directly behind her, knowing that if she wanted to, she could stand up and see me, but she won't. This work is too precious to her. Her lovely ass is in the air hidden by the black cotton, and I know that if I wanted to, I could grab it, touch it, make it my own.

I look at the page in my hand. The story title hangs above an illustration; a large beast, snarling. He stands hunched in front of a smaller woman who wields a knife. On closer inspection, I notice his wounds, his eyes full of pain and fear, not wrath. It is the girl who is shedding tears, inflicting pain on the beast. There is something about the picture that irks me, stirs something uncomfortable inside me, and I place the page on that chair directly in front of her face.

"'Read," I snarl and hear her intake of breath, the crackling of the fire and the crinkle of the leather as her grip tightens.

She begins.

'The Real Beast.'

'Once upon a time, in a land far away, a young prince lived in a shining castle. He was kind, selfless and giving. One dark winter's night a beautiful princess arrived at the castle.'

My hand flies back gathering strength and lands on the perfect roundness of her ass. The smack reverberates in the room. She chokes on her words and stops reading, her head begins to turn toward me. "Look ahead!" I growl at her, and her head snaps back to the paper. She stands there, her breaths heavy, head down, ass up, the silence all-consuming. "I didn't tell you to stop."

"Um." She stammers and begins to breathe through her mouth, low controlled breaths of a person trying to avoid panic.

"Jinx, start reading."

'An enchanting creature that was able to possess the kind prince and wield him to her will.'

My hand comes down a second time, the sound filling the room. This time, though she shivers, she doesn't stop.

'The young prince did everything the enchantress desired, despite knowing much of what she wished for was cruel and sadistic.'

A third smack. She lets out a long breath and continues.

'One night when she approached, he covered his eyes, not wishing to look at her beautiful face, hoping he could break the hold she had over him so that he could protest.'

Again. Again. Again.

She doesn't notice it, but that time her back arches slightly and her ass rises just an inch towards me in invitation. I bet that if I ran my hand along her pussy I'd find her soaked. The thought delights me. Maybe I'm not the only one hiding things in this house.

'The consequences for his refusal would forever change him...'

My hand lands on her plump, reddened ass and this time lingers for a few seconds longer than they should. My fingers trace the hot flesh along the panty line, and she gives up a choking sound like she isn't sure whether to laugh or cry, and I am consumed by a deep dark desire to slip my fingers around the fabric and snatch it from her body, violate her in cruel and terrible ways. But of course, I can't. The thought thrills through me, spreading anger inside my already frustrated body. I snatch my hand away.

She stops reading, the room stands silent apart from her

broken pants, and I realise that that's all she has, for more of the story is contained on the next page.

"Come back tomorrow. Four PM sharp. Wear a skirt." I snarl at her as I rush from the room wishing for the aggravating sensation that has buried itself under my skin to release me. I hear the front door slam, and I suck in a long harsh breath. I know exactly who the real beast is.

9

JINX

"Omission is the most powerful form of lie" – George
Orwell

E verything stops.

Motion. Sound. Breath.

My heart pounds as I sit in my car staring at the house and clutching the two sheets of paper he returned to me. My ass burns where his large palms landed and my cheeks heat. *What the hell was that?*

I replay the last twenty minutes in my head and heat burns my face and ears as adrenaline floods my veins reliving each frightful moment. My hands shake and I grip the steering wheel like a life raft, waiting for the fear to leak out of me. Though I felt vulnerable and helpless, he did not hurt me. I take long steady breaths settling my galloping heart. He still has a hold of me, even though he is in his house and I'm away from him.

That first spank was jarring, unexpected, painful, and the sting it left behind leaked into my cheeks, spreading like a virus stretching the indignation all through my body. But he didn't care; each spank landing perfectly on my ass, drawing out the pain, as if he was punishing me for something I didn't even do.

I shake off the eerie feeling and make my way home, where I tuck away the two pages safely and jump in the shower, washing away the ugly sensation that's stuck to my body like day-old gum.

Lying in my bed I can't help but relive the afternoon in my mind over and over. The searing in my ass when his palm met my flesh, his reaction when it was all over, the anger in his voice, the rustling of his clothes as he stormed out of the room. I try to put the pieces together. Anxiety chewing at my skin as I wonder what tomorrow might bring.

Anger flares inside me and I don't know if it's the humiliation of it all or that I allowed it in the first place, or that maybe a small piece inside me enjoyed it. I shake my head, putting it down to the rush of endorphins flooding my body to protect me from my panic. I go over my options again – I can't seem to find any.

My phone's ringtone pulls me from my thoughts.

"Hello?"

"Hi, Jinx, I hear you've decided to take the job with Mr. Stone." *Mr. Stone*. The name sits heavily on my chest.

"Mr. Stone?"

"Yes, Dorian Stone. He said you will be working with him daily, so I took the initiative and removed you from the weekly schedule." Amanda's voice is sickly sweet.

He what? "I..."

"Fantastic, I'll be in touch." She hangs up before I manage to say anything else.

Who the hell does he think he is? Clawing his way into my life like that, making decisions and forcing my hand. I throw the blanket over my head and try to push away my agitation till I fall asleep.

|||

I pull up to the house beneath the grey angry sky and walk through the courtyard lined with the beautiful blooming roses, and up to the gaping door that swallows me whole. Of course, he's there, waiting, hiding like the cockroach he is, and he sets me to work. This time he has me remaining in the hallway, cleaning the walls and pulling away the cobwebs from the high ceiling. Cold seeps beneath my skin and the glow of the fire from the next room mocks me.

As he did the day before he offers me the chance to earn a second page, as long as I read my work out to him. I don't understand why he wants this. Yesterday he rushed out of the room as if my words offended him, and clearly, my very presence in his house irks him, and yet he's forcing us to remain together longer than necessary. Of course, I accept his offer. It's not like I have any choice. I need my work back.

Reluctantly, I walk over to his seat and bend over like a dog.

The short black skirt I wear rides up my ass, and I feel more exposed. His large body comes to stand behind me, blocking the hot fire from heating my skin.

"Read," he snarls.

My words float in the otherwise silent room as I retell my version of the story, a version where the prince pays the price for being good and kind. Where he is transformed into a feared and hunted beast, and despite his good heart and good intentions, he is chased and broken till his heart freezes over and he learns that goodness doesn't always triumph, and to survive he needs to be calculating and ruthless. He needs to become the monster he was cursed to be. By the time I am done my nerves are strained harp-strings ready to snap at a touch.

The agonising wait for his palm to land a devastating blow against my skin is unbearable, but it never comes. He just stands there, behind me, a harsh looming presence.

The silence hovers over us like a threatening cloud. I don't dare speak or move. I just wait to be dismissed. It's pathetic and aggravating, but I feel glued to the chair. I can't move till he says the word. Any action on my part without his say-so could lead to utter disaster for me.

"The illustration at the beginning of your story – the young girl in the picture was hurting the beast." His voice is contemplative.

"No, she was saving him. Freeing him. She knew his heart and she loved him."

"She loved a monster?" he scoffs.

"The monster was just his skin, his outer shell, but inside, in his heart, there was goodness, beauty, love."

He scoffs at my explanation. "That's where you have it wrong. Monsters don't have hearts." A second later he's rushing towards the door. "Tomorrow, same time, short skirt. Don't be late."

And then, he's gone.

10

JINX

"The tiniest bit of truth made credible the greatest lies."
— Jeffrey Eugenides

My days have fallen into a routine – school, a few hours of trepidation watching the clock tick time away and then *him*. My own personal monster.

I've spent the week cleaning the same two rooms, over and over again. Like he wants to keep me contained or punished. I don't know what his game is, but what I do know, is that at this rate, I won't get all my work back in time. At the end of each session, he has me bend over his chair and read. He hasn't touched me since that first time, but each time I put my hands on the chair the anxiety ties itself inside me in a tight knot of anticipation of something that never comes.

Two pages a day will mean I would have to do this every day for three months. It's not the kind of timeline I can afford. There has to be a way for me to convince him to give me more, quicker.

I wonder what he might ask for if I ask for more pages each day, and how much more I am willing to give him in return. I shudder at the thought as it wriggles inside me like maggots.

Raindrops slash across my windscreen as I pull up to the estate. I'm soaked by the time I walk into the house, even the short run from my car to his front door left me drenched. Walking into the house feels as though I am walking into a walk-in fridge, the large stone walls hold no heat. I stand in a puddle in the hallway, too afraid to move. My teeth chatter as I wait for him to acknowledge my presence.

"You're making my floor wet."

"It's raining outside." *Genius.*

"You have heard of an umbrella?" he throws at me. His condescension winds through my insides, and I clench my fists at my sides.

"I should get to work," I say through chattering teeth.

"Not like that." His voice rings from the darkness.

I look at the empty space in front of me and the large door behind me. "I'm not giving up a day of work because I'm a little wet. I need my pages back."

There's a short silence, and for the first time, I detect a small movement in the shadows, giving me somewhere to focus. "I will bring you a towel. You may dry by the fire before you begin."

"Thank you." The cruel cold filters its way beneath my numbing skin and wraps itself around my bones till my body can do little more but shiver.

"Do not move."

Footsteps echo into the house, and I stand in the hallway, holding myself, trying to find warmth inside my own body.

"I have brought you a towel. Turn around, strip and go stand by the fire, leave your clothes on the floor."

"What? No!"

"See you tomorrow. Same time., Don't be late."

Panic slithers inside me. I can't afford to lose a day's worth of papers, and I was hoping to ask for some more each day. If I piss him off... "Wait."

"For?"

"Just give me the towel," I spit through clenched teeth.

"You're very rude for someone who isn't in a position of power."

I shut my eyes and take a long breath in. *Asshole*. I have the feeling he derives way too much pleasure from playing this game with me. "Can I have the towel, *please*."

"Better. Now turn around and close your eyes."

I do as I'm told. My ears prick up as I strain to listen to movement. There's a brief rustle of clothes and what could be shoes on the stone floor and then there is silence again.

"Open your eyes."

I blink them open. There is a towel a few feet from me, resting on the floor.

"Strip."

"Are you going to watch?" I swallow the lump that gathers in my throat as I slowly turn away.

"Yes."

"I don't want you to." I look down at my hands, my fingertips purple as my teeth keep chattering uncontrollably.

"Are you *certain*?"

I know what he is doing. He's testing how far I'm willing to go, giving me an ounce of power to play with in his twisted game. How many pages would my nudity earn me? What is my dignity worth?

I clear my throat, my eyes sink to my feet. "How many pages will that earn me? Letting you watch."

"Two."

"Two?" My strained voice catches in my throat.

"Take it or leave it, *Jinx*." He draws out my name, and a shiver runs along my back.

"Fine." My reluctance is audible.

"When you are done, go warm yourself up by the fire."

"Thank you." My eyes remain glued to the towel as I suck in air trying to get my brain to make sense of what is happening.

I want to scream, but I don't. Instead, I inhale a stealing breath and begin. My soaking jacket lands on the floor with a wet smack, next I peel my singlet off my body. For a second, it feels almost warmer without the drenched fabric clinging onto it. I drag my skirt down my legs. Goosebumps erupt over my flesh, and I fight the urge to reach for the towel.

"Slow down." His voice comes from the shadows. I feel the heat of his stare, and it cools my skin.

"That's not what we agreed," I throw back to the room. When there are no arguments, my hands slip behind me and I unclasp my bra, letting it slide down my arms. My thumbs hook into my underwear, and I chuck them off before grabbing the towel and covering myself up. I never agreed to pose. As soon as I wrap it around myself, I bolt towards the hearth where the fire is burning, the heat finally leaching into my skin.

I don't know how long I wait, my body toasting by the warm fire before he's there again.

"Better?"

I startle. "Yes, thank you." I clutch the towel tighter around my body, feeling his eyes on me. "Did I earn my pages?"

"I've put your clothes to dry, you should be able to start work soon." He ignores my question, and irritation sweeps through me.

"Thank you. About that..." I chew on my lip looking around the room.

"Yes?"

"I need five more pages each day."

"I see."

"It's just that... three months to earn them all back is too long. I still have to edit and type everything all up..."

"How would you like to earn seven pages a day?"

I do quick maths in my head. If I earn my pages at that rate, I'll only have to endure this man for four more weeks. That would still give me enough time to get it all done in time. "I could do *this* for you." I wave at my body awkwardly, and he scoffs at my weak offer.

"That's not enough."

I chew my lower lip. My stomach tightens and aches. "What would be enough?"

"Stay."

I frown at his words. "What do you mean?"

He sighs, a long, exaggerated breath, as if talking to an idiot. "I mean that you would stay here, with me, as my guest. You will be allowed to leave for your scheduled classes, and the rest of the day will be spent here, at the house."

"You mean, move in?"

"You will have your own wing, and you will continue to clean for two hours each day."

"I... wait... this isn't what I—"

"I'll give you two minutes to consider my offer. After that, it will be off the table. Permanently."

"This is crazy. You can't be asking me to do this. I don't even know what you look like."

"Trust me when I say, that is entirely for your benefit," he hisses, making my stomach roll.

"Can we talk about it?"

"No. This is not a negotiation."

I want to step back, but the fire crackles behind me. Panic snakes inside my body, settling in my belly, and nausea claws its way up my throat. All I want to do is run out of the front door and never return again. I shouldn't have let him watch me strip. None of this should be happening right now, but he has my fucking work.

"What will I have to do? While I'm here?"

"Whatever I say."

A million disjointed thoughts cascade inside me like a waterfall. Hundreds of scenarios play out in microseconds as a cold sweat breaks around my body. My clammy hands clutch the towel as if it's the last fabric of sanity still in this room.

"You can't jus—"

"One minute." His voice hacks through my unrelenting thoughts, but no matter how hard I look, no matter how hard I search for an alternative or an escape route, all I find is a hard wall on which I can bang my fists or head.

"Ten, nine, eight..." His voice taunts me. "Seven, six, five..." I can't fucking do this. I shake my head frantically. "Four, three, two—"

"Fine, yes fuck, I'll do it."

"Do what exactly?"

"I'll move in, till I earn all my pages back."

"And not a day longer."

"Fine." I suck in a long breath to settle my frantic heart-beat. "I just have to go home and ge—"

"No. This is your home now."

"But I nee—"

"Are you reneging on our deal?"

"No, but—"

"Everything you need will be provided for you."

"I—"

"You will stay in the west wing. You may explore the house, but be sure to stay out of east wing."

"The west wing?"

"Yes, up the stairs and to the *left*." He's patronising again.

"Okay."

"I'll get your dry clothes. You can do your chores, then find your room. Dinner is at six."

"Thank you," I bite out. My gaze falls to the floor where I find a little white speck. I focus on it, feeling just as small, just as insignificant, just as dirty. As if to mock me, a light draft picks it up, and it floats up and away, vanishing into the shadows, and I wonder if, at the end of all this, that's where I'll also end up.

11

JINX

"Hurt me with the truth but never comfort me with a lie."
— Erza Scarlet

I'm getting a vibe that my mysterious host is a patronising fuck. Despite not answering any of the questions directly, he did use the word guest, but with him holding my paper hostage, I feel more like a prisoner.

Either way, I have no choice but to play nice. For now.

He did just as he said, leaving my dry clothes for me to wear before having me clean the same room yet again. My hands are stained with brown polish and the smell is beginning to nauseate me. I'm still trying to work out the point of all this.

When he releases me from my duties, he sends me up to my room without the usual reading. There are too many unanswered questions and my skin prickles with unease as I open the door to the bedroom in the west wing.

This place is like somewhere out of a movie set, one with a lavish and exuberant budget. The bedroom is four times the size of my entire apartment yet, despite the size, it feels cosy. A huge four-poster bed is pushed against the opposite wall. Next to it, a cushioned loveseat, and sealed doors on either side of it. Directly in front of me are two double doors laced with windows that open to a balcony. I step closer to the windows which are getting lashed by frozen rain and peer out. Dark clouds blanket the distant mountains, which loom over the gardens beneath. On a calm day it must be beautiful; today it just piles onto the dread that tugs and begs me to run. But to where?

I shake off the feeling – knowing it will undoubtedly slither back along my body – and open the wooden doors. They lead into a walk-in closet, endless shelving and hanging space. Who even has that many clothes? Not me.

I pause. A slow realisation trickles inside me. I don't have *any* clothes besides the one's I'm already wearing.

I set that aside as yet another problem to deal with later and step out of the closet. The other door is a bathroom. It's modern and stark and cold and doesn't fit in with the rest of the house. Frosted grey tiles and an all-glass shower cubicle. Like it's made to make the user feel exposed. I step out and lay on the bed, staring up. Long timber beams traverse the high ceiling. I huff, feeling like a kid who's been sent to her room. I'm still trying to piece together everything I heard and thought I saw, everything that's happened in the last two and a half hours.

Before I have time to dwell, my stomach rumbles again, and I look at the small clock sitting by my bedside. Almost six. Dinner time

I inch my way back to the hallway, enter the door on the right, through to a beautiful modern kitchen with grey marble worktops and state-of-the-art appliances. Like the bathroom, it doesn't belong. I open the fridge to find it stocked with a variety of fruit, dairy and cold meats. I snatch a handful of grapes and feel like a thief before shutting the door and finding the dining room. A curtain has been raised in the room, dividing the table in half. A single plate sits on one side of the curtain.

When I go to peek at the other, a strong hand grips my wrist and pulls it away. My heart falters and kicks up as I turn to see a strange man standing behind me. He is tall and broad, and his dark eyes spear me as he shakes his head.

I yell, yanking my arm, but he doesn't release me.

"Must you scream?" Dorian's voice startles me; he sounds like a rusted tin can.

I suck in a deep breath and stare at the stranger. "Sorry, I just..."

"I guess you've met Victor."

"Victor?"

"Sit down," Dorian answers in his bored angry tone.

The man releases me, and I draw in a ragged breath. I take my seat, my heart flutters in my chest. Has this man always been here? Has he also been watching? What the hell is going on? As I drown in a new puddle of murky questions, I eye the veil that separates my host and me. "Is this curtain really necessary?"

"Only if you want to eat. However, if you prefer to dine *alone*, that can be arranged." I don't miss the threat that the offer carries with it.

"It's fine." I wonder what his definition of 'alone' would be.

My foot taps on the floor as rain taps the windows and the giant clock in the lounge ticks time away. I smell food.

Somewhere in the house, a clock strikes six times. Victor appears. He places a bowl of stew in front of me. The thick steamy broth teeming with meat and root vegetables bobbing around the liquid. Three slices of thinly crusted bread and a small bowl of rice all make my mouth water.

"Thank you." I give him a grateful smile, and he nods as he disappears behind the curtain.

The clank of plates being placed down and the clatter of cutlery gives me permission to start my meal. My spoon sinks into the thick hearty stew, and the flavours explode over my tongue. My grateful stomach screams for more as I shovel spoonfuls into my mouth.

"It's delicious, thank you," I say to the empty part of the room. My reply – the occasional slurp and the clink of spoons against bowls.

"So, what are you doing out here, in this house?" I decide that anything is better than this unrelenting silence.

"Is your room sufficient?" He dodges my question, and I clench my jaw in irritation.

"It's lovely, thank you, but there's not much to do."

"You mean after you finish your studies and chores?"

Muscles tick along my jaw, and I swear my eye twitches. I remain silent.

"Do you like to read?" he offers.

I huff out a reluctant yes.

"I'll have a few books brought up to your room. Any preferences?"

"Anything good."

"Noted, though I doubt we share the same tastes." His condescension is not lost on me. "Anything else?"

"Clothes."

He clicks his tongue, and the sound fills the empty space. "Of course. I'll arrange for a few things for you to wear. I can't have you walking around dressed like you are."

"What? With a shirt and a skirt – that *you* asked me to wear?"

"That shirt is very tight."

My fist grips my spoon too tightly and my knuckles

blanch. Who the hell does this guy think he is? I suck in a long breath and push my anger aside. "Excuse me?"

"And that skirt has seen better days."

I grind my teeth at the insult. "I just haven't gotten around to buying new ones."

"Excuses."

"Fuck you! Who the hell do you think you are?" I shout at the stupid curtain, wanting to tear it down and use my spoon in violent, brutal ways.

"Your host," is all he says before I hear his cutlery kissing his bowl as he continues his meal.

I lean back into my chair, seething, his threat from earlier ringing in my ears. Suddenly eating alone doesn't sound so bad. My appetite dissipates as I look at the steam rising off the chunks of meat. I want to decorate the wall with the fucking stew, but I'm rooted to my chair. I suck in a few calming breaths and try again. "You didn't actually answer my question. What are you doing here?"

He replies with silence. *Asshole.* I refuse to give up.

"Are you hiding?"

Still nothing but the sounds of bodies shuffling in chairs.

"What are you running from?"

"Watch yourself." His tone is sharp and unapologetic. "Despite what you might assume, my hospitality will only extend as far as your behaviour."

"What the hell does that mean?" A shiver runs along my spine.

"It means that if you act like an animal, I'll treat you like one."

"Are you going to hurt me?" I steady my voice and clasp my hands together to stop the sudden shaking.

"What kind of monster do you take me for?"

That's not a real answer, and I'm left to ponder the meaning of his last words.

The curtain rips open, and Victor brushes by me. He eyes my half-eaten soup. I hand the bowl over to him and he frowns.

"It's fine, thank you."

He turns away and disappears with the dishes.

"Why doesn't Victor speak?"

"You'll have to ask him that yourself." Dorian barks a long savage laugh. I'm obviously missing the joke. The one thing that is becoming abundantly clear is that this guy is a psycho, and I need to get the hell away from this place.

I sit listening to him slurp his stew till I can't take it anymore and need to cover up his noise with more noise, human noise.

"Is there much to do here during the day?"

"That depends on who you ask and what you like doing."

More vague answers. "What do you do?"

"Research."

"What are you researching?"

"Why are you studying an arts degree?" he prods.

"Why do you keep dodging my questions?"

"Am I?"

I sigh loud enough for him to hear me and roll my eyes at the stupid curtain. He must hear me cause his voice is almost kind.

"When the weather is better you can explore the garden in the back, till then there are your chores and reading."

"You don't have a computer?"

He doesn't say anything, as if his first statement was enough.

"I need to type up my work, I—"

"I'll have a typewriter sent up to your room."

"A typewriter? This isn't the middle ages."

"Of course not, typewriters were only first available in the late 1800s."

I clench my teeth and blow out a long breath. This guy is getting dangerously close to getting stabbed, damned the consequences. I try one last time. "When will the storm clear?"

"A day, possibly two."

"Two days? What am I meant to do the entire weekend?"

"You have books, you have a room, you have a body and a brain, if you put all those things together you might just come up with something."

"I—"

"Was there anything else?"

There is *so* much else. I want to know who my mysterious host is and why he keeps to the shadows, what he thinks my new schedule should be and how he expects me not to go home at all and retrieve at least some of my things. A million questions whirl in my head that I don't know where to begin. Not that it matters; he's not answered a single one of them anyway.

I can only guess he takes the ensuing silence as my answer.

"Good." He inhales. "Dinner is at six *every* night in the dining room, the clothes and books will be in your room shortly. Tonight you will read for me here."

"Here?"

"Yes, you will read to me while I eat my dessert."

"What about my dessert?"

"You didn't finish your meal."

I stare at the fabric, my eyes trying to penetrate through. *How the fuck could he possibly know that?*

"Now, as we are both done with our main meal, I suggest you stand up and bend over the table."

"What? Now?"

"Did I stutter?"

"What about Victor?"

"What about him?"

"He could—"

"Yes, he could." His voice is sharp and slices through my pounding heart.

"That's not what we agreed to."

"Are you sure? Remind me, Jinx, what were your exact terms?"

"I – em...' I bite down on my lower lips. "You didn't give me a chance to make any."

"You had two minutes."

"To agree!"

"And you did, so now that we have once again established that, stand up and bend over the fucking table. Don't make me ask you a third time."

I stare at the fabric for what feels like a full minute before my legs find the strength to pick my body up and out of my chair. My hips bend at the joints and then my hands are on the table as I lean forward on my arms, the skirt once again riding up my legs. My heart thunders through my chest and my only comforting thought is that he hasn't touched me since that first time when I read him the story of the beast. He only stood there, close. A shiver runs up my spine.

There's a scuffling, and the curtain vibrates with movement before I feel him behind me. One of my pages lands on the table, and I reach out to grab it. "No," he hisses from behind me. "The page stays there."

There is a quickening inside me as I understand what he wants. I swallow the lump in my throat as I shuffle forwards so that my hips touch the edge of the table and my entire torso is leaning on the hard wooden surface.

I grip my page, so this can be over with.

"Not yet." He growls at me in that animalistic way of his, and the paper falls out of my hand. "Reach back and lift up your skirt."

I settle my forehead on the wooden table, feeling my hot shallow breath coming back to me as it bounces off the wood. My breasts squish against the hard table, compressing my already tight chest. *I can't do this.* But I do it anyway, reaching back and gathering the fabric, slowly, dragging it along my skin as if it was an anchor.

"All the way up, over your ass," he says, and my heart drops.

I do as I'm told.

"Move your legs apart," he says, tapping my ankle. I shuffle a little. "More," he hisses, and my legs move apart, pushing my torso flatter onto the surface.

When I am done there is nothing for long sticky seconds. I yelp when I feel the touch of his rough hands on my skin. He growls but says nothing as his fingers hook under the waistband of my underwear and he tugs, pulling them down, stretching them over my ass and hips till they settle like a cotton bridge between my thighs. Cold air touches everything.

"I'm ready for my dessert," he says, and Victor's heavy boots echo on the stone floor.

Heat prickles my skin and my heart stammers. I am fully aware of my ass and pussy being on full display. I clench my eyes shut and wait for whatever comes next. I agreed to this; it's just bare skin, it's nothing at all.

I gasp when something cold lands on the small of my back and then Victor is gone again. Dorian drags a chair over. He sits down and tucks himself in between my legs. He is wide, and my legs pull apart, the underwear digging into my skin. I can feel his breath now, hot and heavy just above my ass.

"Read," he says as the bowl on my back tips a little and he digs his spoon inside.

I grip the page and look at the words, trying to make sense of them. Willing my eyes to focus, for my mouth to work and my voice to breach my lips and make sound, but nothing happens.

"Read, Jinx. I won't ask again."

I clear my throat, acutely aware of his breath on my skin and his proximity, the way his muscular legs push against mine. I fight the urge to turn, to see the monster who holds me captive, and I begin to read. "*Once upon a time there lived a piece of wood...*"

I read the story as Dorian eats his dessert. Each time his teaspoon digs into the bowl, my stomach drops and my heart flutters, but I continue reading.

I freeze as a drop of cold ice cream lands on my ass. It leaks slowly down, edging its way between the two cheeks.

"I didn't tell you to stop," he says as the cool sensation leaks further down.

I chew on my lower lip for a few seconds before I continue.

A second drop of ice cream follows the path of the first. The teaspoon digs into the bowl.

"*On a dark night when the moon was veiled by the clouds and only a single star peeked through the blanket of clouds, the old man made a wish that his creation would come alive and become the boy he'd never had.*" I stop.

"Why did you stop?" His voice hums over me.

"I'm done, this is all I have."

"Mm, mm."

My breath catches in my throat when his finger connects with my skin. It feathers over me and traces the path of the fallen ice cream, collecting it as it runs in the opposite direction. My inner thigh, between the cheeks of my ass and over the swell, before it vanishes. I listen to his soft groan as he sucks at his finger. My heart shivers.

Without another word, his chair drags across the floor, and I know he's gone.

I swivel around finding an empty room. I rip the bowl off my back, pull up my underwear, lower my skirt and run up to my room.

I launch myself onto the bed and scream into the pillow. My warden is an arrogant self-righteous piece of shit. Frustration swims through me like a swarm of eels, their angry stings jolt through my body, making my skin burn. I roll onto my back and catch my angry breaths. How could I have been so stupid?

12

DORIAN

**"Of all the lies I've heard 'I love you' was my favourite." —
Alok, Felix Jaehn & The Vamps**

From my vantage point, I have a perfect view of the bed. She's adequate when she sleeps, her delicate features rising and falling. I wish she wasn't curled up so tightly, that her grip would loosen on the blanket so that I could see her chest move. The beating of her heart.

Every time she stirs and kicks out, she moans a little, and that wonderful, strange sensation awakens my body. She's obviously having a nightmare; her face pulls into tiny frowns as her closed eyes squeeze tight.

She moans again and that flaccid useless cock of mine that hasn't worked in years twitches. It doesn't stand or harden, but it feels *something*. And that's a start.

I stare at this girl from the tiny peephole and draw in a long breath, savage thoughts swirling inside my head.

I tear myself away and pause to gather myself before I

take my leave. Maybe this time things will turn out differently.

|||

JINX

The monster chases me through the woods. I feel his breath on my neck when he whispers my name. I run for my life. My legs get heavier and each step becomes harder. The monster reaches out, his long nails brushing against my skin.

My eyes tear open, and I scramble up the headboard of the bed, my breath coming in sharp inhales. My forehead is peppered in cold sweat and chills run up my body. I haven't had a nightmare in years. This place brings bad things to the surface. My singlet clings to my body in sweaty clumps. I feel dirty again. The kind that's hard to wash away. I need a shower. But for that, I'd need clean clothes.

Dim grey light spills through a slit in the curtain. I look around the room to find a pile of clothes on the love seat. A shiver runs along my spine. *Someone's been here while I slept.* I scramble off the bed, my hands wrapping themselves around my chest, clinging to my arms as my eyes sweep the room. I can't shake the feeling of being watched.

I need more light to drown away these dark feelings. Drawing the curtains, I discover that the rain has eased off outside, and it's now a delicate patter that kisses the window. My gaze sweeps the room as light touches every corner. There's no one here but me.

On the love seat, I wade through the pile of clothes and

sigh. Oversized t-shirts and button-ups are all sealed in plastic, still new. The same goes for the pack of too-large boxers that rests next to them.

Great.

I grab a fresh shirt and boxers from the pile and head for the shower.

||||

DORIAN

She stares at herself in the mirror, pulling at her tired skin and running her hand through her frazzled hair. She's a mess and she knows it. She sighs, maybe in disgust or maybe she knows she will never amount to anything more, be any more beautiful. I applaud her. Being honest with herself will only help her in the long run.

Before all this, a girl like her would still be on the menu for me. I'd chew her up and spit her out like the junk food she is, knowing that even if I don't allow myself to swallow, I know she'd leave a delicious fucking taste on my tongue. That's the thing about junk food; there's an outlet around every fucking corner – it's cheap, accessible and everywhere – just like girls such as her. This girl was part of a very special herd. I bet she would have done anything for me.

The thought, as always, only makes me angry and despondent. I shake it off and wait. Jinx turns the water on. Steam rises and creates a veil on the mirror, obscuring my view, but only for a second. The anti-fog coat on the mirror doesn't allow the water to cling. Jinx tests the water. She flinches a number of times before she's satisfied.

Grabbing the hem of her singlet, she peels it from her body. Her hip bones protrude from her black underwear, and warmth travels inside me like I've woken up after a long hibernation. It's odd and uncomfortable and I resist the urge to scratch. She sheds her underwear, leaving a thin red circumference around her slim hips.

I stare intently at this creature that has invaded my home. Despite her face, her body is delightful. Lovely perky tits that would fit perfectly into my palms. They bounce a little as she moves to remove her underwear. My gaze lands on the patch of black hair at the apex of her thighs and my body lurches. It aches. Waking from its long ugly slumber.

When she isn't scared and stiff, she flows, like the water – she moves gracefully. She's so much lovelier when she doesn't know she is being watched. I lick my lips, wanting to taste her. I'll get my chance.

The water runs in long translucent streams over her delicate body. Her white skin blushes with the heat, her nipples stiffening underneath a lather of soap. I have an urge to be that water, to run along her body, to invade all of her space. Be the reason her nipples are hard.

The soap gone, her flesh pink, I notice for the first time the raised white marks. Long white scars on her knees. Imperfect. Of course. I knew not to expect anything else. She pats herself dry, drops the towel and reaches for the boxers, dragging them over her short legs.

She turns to study herself in the mirror. They hang loosely over her hips. So loose they trickle down with her movements. She sighs, and I grin, willing them to fall completely away. I don't like her covered up. Maybe permitting her clothes was a mistake.

She finds her hairband and ties the end of the boxers in a ball, tightening them around her. She looks ridiculous and sexy with her naked breasts and her damp hair and those boxers forced into place. She shucks a black t-shirt on, and I note the absence of her bra. I bite down on my lower lip as an old sensation ripples through me.

She studies herself for another moment before leaving the bathroom, leaving me to wonder what else she might awaken inside me.

||||

JINX

After my shower, I look over the books he left for me. An eclectic mix of classic and modern literature. I read through the titles seeing a few familiar names, but my gaze lands on a book about halfway through the pile. It's thick and compact, the cracked spine embedded with delicate and ornate ornaments. I pull it from the pile and run my fingers over the worn leather cover. A composition of creatures and elements has been carefully carved and dyed into the leather and in the middle emblazons a red and green title which has faded to obscurity over the years.

My heart lurches when there is a knock at my door. I pull the shirt down over the boxer shorts and stand in the middle of the room like an idiot.

"You have two hours to complete your chores." His voice slithers from beneath the door and crawls over my flesh leaving a trail of goosebumps in its wake.

"Now?"

I'm greeted with silence and take his non-answer as yes. After slipping on that ridiculous skirt, I make my way back down to the hallway where I find the cleaning supplies.

Like an idiot, I once again clean the same small space, dusting the surfaces that are no longer covered in dust, filling the space with the pungent sweet smell of wood polish as I go over the now shining surfaces yet again. I don't get this. I do not get any of this, or his need for my services when he clearly has someone else here, living with him, cooking and what else? The thoughts plague me as my body moves in automatic motions, repeating what it did the day before.

|||

"You're done." His voice comes out of the dark and startles me.

"Shit," I whisper to myself as my heart lurches into my throat. "Stop doing that."

"Doing what?" He plays coy. "If you want your second page, clean up and come read for me."

"Wait."

"What is it?"

"Can I get some breakfast?"

"Something can be arranged, now hurry up."

He's gone, leaving me to pack away the few bottles and rags I've used. I wonder why he's always in a hurry. What the hell does he do all day?

When I get back into the lounge I can feel him, and like a well-trained dog, I go over to the chair and bend, waiting for his next command.

"Look down, till you're told otherwise." My body shivers as I do. Last night plays back in my head; the way his finger traced my skin. The way it felt. It felt terrible and frightening, and incredibly fucking good all at the same time. Just a taste of sensation.

I do as I'm instructed and look at the perfect leather seat, my grip tight. I feel him beside me when he puts my plate down.

"You may eat."

I look beside me to find a bowl of grapes. It's an odd choice for breakfast food. I was hoping for coffee and toast. I draw in a long breath and pluck a grape from the vine before sucking it into my mouth and chewing. Its sweet juice explodes all over my tongue, and I find myself reaching for another before I finish the first. I eat five grapes before I stop. I feel his eyes on me, burning through my skin. He's watching me eat. I shudder at the realisation and push the bowl away.

"I'm done."

"If you say so. Eyes down."

He removes my plate, setting it aside. Am I being punished for not wanting him to watch me?

"Read," he says, and I look up to find my pages where the bowl was. I grab them and clutch them to my chest as if trying to convince myself they are real.

"Just five?"

"Two for your chores, and the three you are owed for staying half a day yesterday, the five owed to you for today you will receive tomorrow morning."

"Thank you," I stammer as tears spring to my eyes. The absurdity of paying my way to earn what is mine claws at my brain, obscuring right from wrong. Why did I agree to this? Surely I could have just told someone. Except…

His heat burns my skin as he stands behind me. "Pull up your skirt."

My hands shake as I reach behind me and slowly bunch the fabric. Somehow it feels worse me doing it, like I'm okay with it, like I have given him permission.

"Now the underwear," he growls in his deep voice.

I tug at the hairband holding them in place to rip it

away. The fabric unravels, and the boxers fall easily from me, pooling at my feet.

His intake of breath has my heart squirming in my chest.

"Read, Jinx."

Swallowing, I flip my pages and start reading, continuing the story from last night.

"*As the old man took his warm whiskey and tucked himself in for the night falling into a deep slumber, a fairy descended upon the dark room and sat by the boy, caressing his face.*"

My voice stutters when the snick of his zipper cuts through my words and silences them.

"I didn't tell you to stop." He sounds strained, and I clear my throat.

Fumbling with the pages, I find my place and continue. As the words spill from my mouth, he begins. At first, I am uncertain, but as his breathing speeds up and the shadows around the room move, I am sure of it. He is touching himself behind me, tugging violently on his cock. My words bleed out in broken phrases as his breathing speeds up. I choke and splutter around the words that no longer want to come.

"Read!" he growls through a strained pant, and I hurl out the story, spewing it into the room to hide his harsh, strangled breaths. When I am done, I fall silent, waiting for the hot cum to coat my back, waiting for his long groan of pleasure. Instead, all I get is anger.

"Your stories are ridiculous!" he growls. "Dinner is at six," he reminds me as he storms from the room.

"Then why do you keep asking me to read them to you?" I shout after him, but of course, I'm only answered with silence. I pull up my clothes, my hands shaking. What the fuck was that?

DORIAN

F*uck.*

I was so close that time it was like chasing a shadow. The sensation was at my fingertips, the closest I've come in years, but still nothing. I kick the decimated chair in the corner of the room, the casualty of all my brute force and punishments over the years. Almost time to get Victor to replace it again.

I pace my room like a violent tumbling storm. Darkness seeps from within me. I'm so close I can taste it and yet, nothing has changed at all.

I kick the chair again.

Fuck.

My thoughts drift back to the last time my cock worked.

I've been exchanging looks with the girl for a few hours. She dances and looks at me as she moves. Pink colours her cheeks every time I smile at her. Despite my new imperfections she still finds me attractive. The last few weeks have been painful. A nightmare. My nose is no longer straight, and my cheekbones seem to have become almost hollow. Still, even with these new inconveniences, I look better than most of the other men here. And then there's my size. Girls like a tall man; they think he will protect them.

It's instinct.

It's the wrong one.

She finally comes over and slides herself between my legs. My cock already hard and throbbing needing release. She's not shy. I like it.

"What's your name?"

"Amber."

"It's a beautiful name." I wince and wait. Nothing happens. I must be telling the truth. It's been so long I'd forgotten. I sigh in relief. She doesn't notice.

"Thanks."

"You like dancing?"

"You like watching?" she winks at me.

I smile. I've learned that with girls sometimes less is more. She can interpret it as she likes. "Would you like to get out of here?"

"What for?"

I swallow and bite my tongue. Afraid.

She starts laughing. "You should see your face." She follows the contour of my jaw with her finger. "Sure. Let's go."

She gives me a reprieve, and I guess I'm still good-looking enough for her standards. They must be low.

I smirk and take her hand leading her to the elevator. She's like everyone else, asking questions and jabbering on. I don't know why girls do it. Perhaps it's because they're nervous or they are looking for a last-minute connection. The nerves I can understand.

I lead her straight to my room. No need for pleasantries or drinks. If she wanted those she should have enjoyed them downstairs.

She cuts away from me and stands at the base of my bed, watching me watching her, slipping the thin strap of her dress off her shoulder. She is trying to be provocative. She's failing miserably. I don't really need a show, just a warm hole to stick my dick. It's painfully hard now as it's been a while and I have my needs, even if I have to lower myself to her standards.

I appease myself knowing I'm probably not going last long anyway.

She smiles as I undo my belt, most likely getting the wrong idea.

"Do you think I'm pretty?" The dress falls from her body, lying in a black pool at her feet. Thank fuck for the dim light.

"Of course, you're the most beautiful girl I've ever seen," I croon as I study her not-so-slim figure. Doesn't matter what she looks like, she is easy prey; mildly attractive and just the right amount of overly desperate.

But even as the lie spills from my mouth, pain prickles my body, like I've woken an army of fire ants and they run beneath my skin. The girl is saying something, but all I can hear is my blood rushing around my body like it's running away from itself.

I push the girl away as pain overwhelms my senses, flooding through me like a hurricane. The angry crack reverberates along my back as my spine tears my body in half and pressure builds inside my skull as my nose erupts. Hot blood gushes between my fingers as I try to hold the liquid and pain at bay. Red rivulets run down my arm and tears burn my eyes.

I fall to my knees, screaming. The girl is also screaming, I think she uses words like freak and asks me what the fuck I'm doing. She might be asking if I'm okay.

After a time the pain subsides, as do my cries. I regain myself on the floor of my bedroom. It's vacant, the girl long gone. A howl breaks free from somewhere inside me, a feral, angry noise that rips from my mouth and echoes against the walls.

My reflection doesn't lie. Though I wish it would. It's been three weeks since I met that deranged woman in the elevator and my world twisted on its head. She stole the best part of me and is punishing me each time I use it.

After my nose broke for the fourth time, I found the pattern. It should have been obvious, of course, but when you think with your dick and not your brain, thoughts get muddled, and old habits do not break as easily as bones.

The man standing in front of me is a monster; my back is no longer straight, and my legs feel like one has become shorter than the other. I cannot walk without shuffling, and when I grit my teeth in anger, the strange uneven fangs slice my lips. I study the odd angle of my nose, no longer sitting on my face with perfect symmetry but rather slicing it at an obscure angle that pulls at my left eye and tugs at my right lip. I keep pulling it back, reminding it where it belongs but to no avail.

By then it became obvious. She'd cursed me.

13

JINX

**"Man is not what he thinks he is, he is what he hides." —
André Malraux**

I've stayed holed up in 'my' room most of the afternoon. Reading is an escape, a place I can run to that isn't here, yet my treacherous body betrays me with the need for food. I drop the book on the bed and edge out of the room and down the stairs, my body alert, despite the stiffness in my muscles.

I stay in the shadows as I make my way down the hallway, enter the door on the right and into the kitchen. I open the fridge, searching for something substantial. A noise startles me and suddenly I feel like an intruder about to be caught. A shiver of panic runs through me. I shut the door and make my way to the dining room, as if that was always my intended destination. The curtain is gone, and I can see the long table that splits the room. It seats twenty-four, and I wonder if it's ever been full to capacity. I wonder if he has enough friends to fill all the spots; if he has any friends at all. I wonder if they all know what a big asshole he is. I play with the idea of enticing one of his guests to take me away from here forever. I shake the thought away, knowing I can walk out of the front door any time I like, I'll just be doing it empty-handed.

I wait a few long minutes until the uneasy feeling of being watched falls away and the silence returns. The house feels deserted again as I return to the kitchen and make myself a small sandwich. I'm hungrier than I thought after dismissing most of my stew the night before and the few pathetic grapes he allowed me for breakfast.

I wash my dishes and set them back in place. Maybe I'm afraid they'd know I was here. I shake the strange feeling. I've never had to cover my tracks before. At least not in my own home. This whole place feels wrong.

My skin crawls with agitation. I'm not used to being cooped up. It makes me feel vulnerable, the four walls close in, taunting me. I walk into the lounge; as usual, it is empty. I return to the hallway and make my way down the corridor till I spot a door and try the handle. I'm surprised when it gives way and I fall into the room as it swings inwards.

I gasp as my gaze sweeps over the room. A library. The walls are stacked with books floor to ceiling and in the middle is a massive table covered with books lying open. Maps and parchment decorate every other flat surface.

Movement catches my eye, and I freeze.

"What are you doing in here?" His voice is a sharp shrill holler as he swivels, and his gloved hands cover his face.

"You said I could explore—"

"Get out!" he screams at me.

"I'm—"

"Get. Out!" It's a ferocious angry roar that makes my bones quake.

I race out and upstairs to my room where I slam my door and lean against it, breathless. Did I see his face? I'm unsure. He was a blur of movements and savage sounds.

A rapping on my door jolts my already faltering heart.

"Jinx?" His raspy voice seeps beneath the wood and strangles me.

"Go away," I choke out, my voice betraying me.

Silence. But I know he's there, I can feel his presence through the door. It feels cold and dangerous.

"I wasn't... expecting you," he says, like it's meant to mean anything. Still sounding angry, unsettled.

"Go away," I repeat, not wanting to listen to him.

"I'm not used to... people being in my home."

Is that his way of apologising? He's pathetic. I push myself harder against the door. My throbbing heart answers in a frantic beat. "I never asked to be here," I remind him.

"Dinner is at six," is all he says.

Warmth creeps back into my body and I know he's gone, and yet it takes me a few long minutes before I can unglue my back from the door and land on the bed.

||||

My stomach grumbles, and I look at the clock. A few minutes past six. As if on cue there's a knock at my door.

"I'm not coming," I call out, and I'm greeted by silence.

He knocks again, and I decide to ignore him. When nothing follows, I guess he's gone.

A few minutes later there's a pounding on my door. "I told you dinner is at six." His irate voice rushes inside the room.

"And I said I wasn't coming."

"Dinner starts at six," he repeats.

I shake my head. "You said I'm not a prisoner, which means I can make my own choices. I choose not to have dinner with you sitting behind your stupid veil and playing stupid games."

"If you don't eat with me, you don't eat at all!" he thunders behind the door, and I shiver at his words.

"Fine!" I shout back.

"Fine." It's like a whisper that slithers across my skin and makes me cold all over again. I crawl under my blanket.

||||

DORIAN

I stab at my steak, watching the blood drain from the meat and collect in a puddle on my plate. A pang of anger shivers through my veins like a strike on a tuning fork. Not only did she almost see me, but like a fool, I went to apologise. Despite all that, she still refused to dine with me. In my home. I grind my uneven teeth and stab at the bleeding meat. Her audacity riles me and anger surges inside me, festering.

I am, after all, doing her a favour. She should be grateful.

I cut the fleshy steak on my plate. The meat tears away from the sinew viciously as I cleave at it, and I think about her damn stories. '*Fairytales and other truths*'. What are these truths meant to be? Why does each one feel like it was written about me? That fucking beast mocked me, and the wooden boy? He didn't even pretend to want this life; he knew not to try to be more than he was. In the end, all that he would have gotten was death anyway. Pathetic.

I push my mostly uneaten meal away and stand up. The chair clatters to the floor behind me. I need to relieve myself of my anger so that it doesn't rot inside me. I've allowed for that before – at the beginning, when things began to change – it only led to more pain.

I tear through the house and go to my room where I push my way through my clothes and find the peephole. I look at the girl who has invaded my space so crudely. She is asleep, and I wonder what she dreams about as she kicks and whimpers. She stirs things in me. Things that have been dormant for so long. Her crudeness and unrefined ways irritate and gnaw at me, but also intrigue me. Her reluctance to join me at my table and respect my rules irks me.

She fell asleep fully dressed, and I find myself irate at the prospect. I want her to sleep in less. I want to see more of her. I want to...

Have her. The realisation sends me reeling, and a jolt touches my cock. Once again it wakes, not fully erect, not functional but aware.

I growl at the woman in the bed. She's doing things to me.

This will not do.

I tear myself away from the peephole, out of the walk-in closet and to my window where I glare at the dark sky. I recall a few of the books I'd read that mentioned women. And I have tried women... so many women, who grimaced at my flaccid cock and put it in their mouth at the prospect of earning a few dollars. But no matter how much they sucked, nothing happened. I remained soft and they ran off, repulsed. Maybe she is different, the one who can break this curse, end my torture and set me free. For good this time.

A trickle of hope slides inside me and I push it down and bury it along with my past. Hope is a dangerous thing for a creature like me. But the feeling niggles, the new possibility lighting a fire that's been all but smouldering embers for the last few years as my hopes were dashed.

I grab the key to the library and step out of the room.

Time to get back to work.

14

JINX

**"Truth is most beautiful undraped." — Arthur
Schopenhauer**

It's the hunger pangs that wake me; a harsh cramp that reminds me I'm still human and can't escape my basic needs. I slip out of bed and creep downstairs. The house is silent as always. I step into the kitchen and freeze. Standing in the dark shadows is a figure. His face whips around to find me, and our eyes lock.

"Why are you down here?"

"I'm hungry," I say.

"Don't come any closer." This time his voice is calm, a lowly husky rumble.

I freeze, not daring to move. I feel his eyes on me; they glow in the dim light, tracking me.

His body shifts and he places something on the counter. I think it's a book and I wonder how he can read so well in such poor lighting. He moves farther into the darkness. "I told you that if you don't eat with me, you won't eat at all."

"You did say that, but then you scared me."

"I wouldn't have scared you if you knocked, like a civilised person."

I ignore the jab. "I didn't realise I had to knock on every door in a house you said I could explore at my leisure."

He doesn't respond for a while, and I think I have finally won an argument against him. I can't help the smug smirk that tugs at my lips. Fuck him.

"I'd like to show you the library."

"No thanks," I manage.

"It will remain unlocked from now on, and I will be... prepared."

I don't know what he means, and I don't care, "whatever."

When he's silent for a while I shuffle forward. A low growl emanates from the shadows, and I stop. "Can I eat?"

"No."

My mouth falls open. "You can't starve me!"

In the shadows, it's hard to see him, but I think I see his broad shoulders shrug. "A few days without food won't hurt you as long as you have water. If you want to eat you will eat with me. Those are the rules, and you will obey them."

"Obey? Like a slave?"

"Like a guest with manners."

"I'm not your guest, I'm your prisoner," I hiss at him.

"What you are, is a victim of your own circumstances and the sooner you accept that the better things will be. For both of us."

"Fuck you, Dorian."

"In due time." My heart drops to the bottom of my stomach at his words, and I swear I can feel his smirk all the way from across the room. "Good night, Jinx." He dismisses me nonchalantly and grabs the book from the counter, turning his back to me.

I want to scream. I want to rush him and claw at his face. I want to eat. Instead, I stomp up to my room like a petulant child and go back to sleep.

|||

JINX

I n the dream, I'm running towards her voice, she calls my name in desperation. The long dark alley turns into a rose garden, red petals falling at my feet as I run. Sharp thorns snatching at my face, wind and lashing rain and *him* behind me, invisible. I feel him even when I can't see him.

I shoot up in the bed and scramble back to the headboard. My heart pounds and my body is covered in sweat. I can still feel him. My stomach churns, but I ignore it.

I breathe. The mechanical nature of inhaling and exhaling relaxes me. I can count the seconds as I draw in a breath and let it out slowly. My heart slows, my tight skin loosens, and I let the blanket that I clutch tightly fall away.

Golden fingers of light play with the edge of the curtains and I bolt from the bed and pull the curtain aside. Sunlight. It streams inside the room like a forest fire, hot and all-consuming.

Running around like a headless beast, I rush to the bathroom, splash my face and pull on some clean clothes. The boxers are too big, but my bra is dry and the oversized shirt falls well past halfway on my thigh.

I run downstairs through the deserted lounge and hall and rush outside where the line of rose bushes paralyses me. My heartbeat accelerates; it's the only thing inside me that can move. For a short eternity, I stand, till I feel him behind me. When I whirl around, the doorway stands empty. I suck in a long breath and run through the lines of roses, sprinting till the tiles become soft mud that squelches beneath my feet and splatters onto my legs. I run and run and run.

My breath catches in my throat when I reach my car and lean against it, letting the sun warm my face. With a light breeze grazing my skin, I feel a sense of freedom. But as I look around, I know it's false. I'm still here, on his land, the long white fence cutting me off from the rest of the world. I know I can walk out at any time, but invisible hooks keep me in place. If I want what's mine, I must remain.

The property is large, a few acres at least, yet it still feels small. Now that it's not raining, the place feels less menacing, beautiful almost. I scan the horizon, the looming mountains casting a shadow over the back gardens.

My thoughts return to the beast in my dreams, an invisible force that makes my heart shudder. It doesn't matter how far I get, monsters always follow me. At least the one inside the house can be seen and felt, maybe even negotiated with. I sigh thinking of our conversation last night and his refusal to allow me an ounce of freedom outside his rules.

It's ridiculous. I agreed to stay over and let him touch me so that I can get my work back, not be subjected to his hideous temper and ridiculous requests. I will not tolerate it. I huff and cross my hands over my chest, puffing it out slightly as I do. I plan on marching right into that house and letting that asshole know he won't get away with it anymore.

I stare at the looming door set like a gaping mouth in the house.

But maybe I'll enjoy the sun a little more first. I lean against my car and close my eyes.

||||

DORIAN

I give myself permission to enjoy the sunshine, if only for a few brief minutes. Watching my new pet enjoy the sun, my fingers idly running over the four deep grooves in the wood. She is a beautiful bird with clipped wings and that makes her precious. She can escape, but she can't fly and that could see her get hurt. Except I can't let that happen. I stare at her for a few more minutes before stepping back inside. Now that I have found hope there's too much at stake. A new plan must be created and pursued with rigorous and austere measures.

I slink down to the library, pausing with the key in my hand. I promised her she could have access to the room. And I'd be lying to myself if I said I didn't want to have her here. Her company awakes things inside me.

I'm lost in research when there's a soft tapping at the door.

"Hello?" She must have had her fill of sunshine and her inability to amuse herself has her seeking something to do. It's almost sad.

"One minute," I call out. Today, I'm ready for her, I'm calm. I am prepared.

I slip on the long black gloves that make my skin itch, don my cloak and a veiled mask that shields my face and stand at the back of the room. There are no shadows to hide behind here; I need light to read. My attire and distance will have to do.

"Come in," I say and watch as the door sways open. It's agonisingly slow like she's still uncertain, but brave and eager. Like a mouse knowing that if it can outsmart the death trap it can still get the cheese. I don't have any more time to ponder the qualities of brave and stupid people because she walks in and is immediately the most interesting thing in the room. Not for any reason other than she is new. The only unexplored source of information.

I watch her. Her gaze sweeps the room until her eyes fall on me. She shivers and her body stiffens. The air is thick in an unsettling silence as her gaze takes me in. Though I am covered, I'm well aware that my morphed shape is no longer entirely human, my hands more like claws and my face elongated and fierce. Her eyes grow wider with each passing moment, and it seems as if she hasn't taken a breath since laying eyes on me.

I give her a curt nod and take a step backwards, extending the distance between us. What else does she want?

My slight movement breaks her sudden paralysis, and she takes it as a gesture of safety or maybe an invitation and inches farther into the room. Her fingers feather the maps strewn on the flat surfaces, her lips falling slightly open as she scans the books and shelves. The sheer volume must be astonishing to someone like her.

"So many books," she says.

I'm not sure if she's talking to me, but I respond anyway. "That's why it's a library."

She rolls her eyes and her lips move. I don't know what she says but I'm fairly sure she is mocking me. I guess it's not surprising. I add immature to her list of poor qualities.

She walks over to the window where the four long

marks scar the woodwork. She fingers the damaged wood, and a jolt shivers inside me. I resist the urge to tell her to move away. "What happened here?"

I can't lie so I stay silent. It's not really her business. When I don't respond she turns away from the window, walks to the desk and begins scanning over the books, picking one up and leafing through the pages.

"Be careful with that."

She ignores me. "What *is* all this?" Her hand sweeps over the table where my books lay open.

"Research."

She does that thing with her lips again. Mocking me.

"Could you be a little more specific?"

"No." I wait. I anticipate she will find the content boring and will leave. Instead, she starts scanning each book in turn, reading but a few pages and dragging her fingers over maps.

"I didn't take you for a magician."

"I'm not." I raise an eyebrow, her assumption taking me by surprise.

"And yet everything here pertains to magic, curses and fairy tales."

"You got that just by scanning a few books?"

"Doesn't take a genius to work it out. And anyway you have a Grimoire sitting right here."

"You know what that is?"

"Why wouldn't I?" She turns towards me, her eyes narrowing.

"Because you're—"

"A girl?" she challenges.

"A housemaid." I don't really answer her question.

She huffs. "Firstly, I'm a cleaner, not your maid, and secondly, my job doesn't define me or tell you anything about me."

"Perhaps. You seem to be more educated than you let on. So then why aren't you doing something—"

"More?"

I shrug. A ghost of a frown crosses her face and I think I see her shiver.

"Why do I need to do more? I'm happy with the job I have. It suits my schedule and pays the bills."

"You clean toilets. Your family must be so proud."

"Keep my family out of this," she snaps, and I can't help the smile that slips across my face beneath my mask. I have obviously touched a nerve. I decide to scratch a little more.

"Why? They don't approve of your choices?"

"I said keep them out of this." The muscles on her jaw tense.

"Why? Because you are embarrassed of them or them of you?" I can't help but keep poking.

"They have no idea where I am or what I do." Her tone is cold and crisp and slices through the hot room. *Interesting*. "So you're hiding?"

"Look who's talking," she throws at me. I note she neither confirms nor denies my question. "A recluse living on a very large, very isolated property worth more than I'd earn in two lifetimes. You have a personal butler, and some of these books are so rare, very few people would have the money or audacity to own them."

"Audacity?"

"They belong in the national library where everyone should have access to them."

I scoff at her words. This woman is delusional. "And what would 'everybody' do with them?"

"What are *you* doing with them?"

"I've already said, research."

"What kind?"

"The personal kind."

"You're not the only one in the world with problems."

"No. But I am one of a few with the financial capacity to do something about them."

She huffs and rolls her eyes at me. "You're also an arrogant, selfish ass who's keeping all this to himself."

She's not wrong. But her attitude is starting to grate against my nerves. She is forgetting her place.

"Will you tell me why you're hiding your face?"

"No." I find myself slightly disappointed at her question. She's seen how my body has become so misshapen, she must have some idea what lies behind my veil.

She sighs, frustration clear across her features. "Well, will you tell me about your research? Maybe I can help."

I snigger then clear my throat to cover up the sound as her eyes narrow and burn into mine like she can see right through my veil. I fight not to take a step back.

"Fine," I say reluctantly, and her face relaxes an inch. "I'm looking for a way to lift a curse."

The tightness around her eyes is back and her lips curl in an angry snarl. "Don't lie to me."

"I couldn't even if I tried." I don't know if she can hear the bitterness in my voice.

"Stop making fun of me." She waits. I like her all twisted up and angry. I shake the thought away. I don't like her at all.

"I'm not." I watch her face as it transforms from anger to a mixture of fear and fascination.

She looks around again, absorbing, believing, but she doesn't understand yet. "What sort of curse. Are *you* cursed? Is the house cursed? Am *I* cursed now too?" She takes a step back, then continues firing questions at me. "Or is it Victor? Wait, is that what you hide? Did something happen to you? Who did you piss off? Probably everyone." She mumbles that last one to herself. "What have you tried already? Has anything worked? Did you make it worse? Can you answer me?"

I'm staring at her, my mouth stretched in an amused smile she can't see. She is very entertaining and certainly inquisitive. "Which one of those questions would you like me to answer?"

"All of them." She looks at me like I'm stupid and that should have been obvious.

"There were just... so many..." I smirk as I watch her become exasperated.

Maybe making little Miss Jinx irritated could be a little side project of mine. It's been a while since I've gotten under anyone's skin. The thought delights me but only for a second. I was never a popular guy. Other men were jealous of me, and women wanted my company for my money or my cock. But I've never had what you might call friends. And when I realised that people only took advantage of me, I found ways to push them away. A few snide comments and belittling remarks. The only time I was nice was when I wanted something. Now I want something again. I want to make this little firework go off. Except I'm not sure if I want her to go off in my library or in my bed.

"I said stop making fun of me." She jolts forward and pushes me. I take two steps back, unprepared for her attack.

My skin crawls and my body flares. "Don't fucking touch me!" I snarl and lunge at her. She rushes back and her back hits the wall. I cage her in with my arms, heat and something almost recognisable crawls through me. I pant above her, growling. Her boldness angers me, makes me feel things.

Makes me feel.

"Don't. Touch. Me," I repeat into her face. I see her fear – taste it. The saucer-like eyes, the way she glues her back to the wall, trying to get swallowed whole. Yet instead of doing what I expect her to do and cower, she rolls her shoulders back and straightens her spine.

"I guess it was an asshole curse. Not even a true love's kiss will break that one. Not that anyone could ever love you." She rips herself from the wall and barges through my hands and out of the library.

I'm left breathless and pissed. But I don't give a shit because my cock hurts. It throbs as it pushes against my pants. It's so fucking hard I think I might explode in my pants. A whirl of emotions tornadoes inside me; anger, delight, thrill, confusion. It's been years. *Years.* I release it from my pants, groaning as I wrap my hand around the aching shaft. I'm not slow, and I'm not gentle. Greedy with need, I need too much.

I'm lost to a sensation so familiar, so foreign, that my head reels. My mouth falls open with a desperate moan as I chase it. I stroke my shaft hard. It's so fucking good. Too good. My whole body shudders as an orgasm rips through me and I cum hard and fast, my knees threatening to buckle and my lungs squeezing. I growl like an animal into the room then roll over leaning against the wall I just decorated with my cum, my cock growing limp in my hands and her words searing my ears. *Not even a true love's kiss will break that one.*

Not that anyone could ever love you.

If only she knew that she isn't entirely right or entirely wrong. I have been loved before, but never enough...

||||

DORIAN

I'm pleased when she shows up for dinner. Finally falling into place. Obeying. Is that what I want from her? Obedience?

No. I'd rather have her fight, I decide. I smirk as I think about my afternoon. I've tried to relive it, to get the blood in my body to flood my cock again, but nothing flares it like she does. So if I wait long enough, I have no doubt she will bring out the best in me as I bring out her worst.

"Hello?" Her usual greeting.

"Thank you for gracing me with your presence." Why delay the inevitable? I want to feel again.

She exhales sharply and glares at the curtain. Her eyes narrow, her lips move silently. Her childish display is amusing. She has no idea I can see her through the fabric. One of my better investments.

Victor brings our food and I dive in, the afternoon exertion having left me drained. I'm famished. But I'm not sure food will fill this new hollow appetite.

"I'm sorry about this afternoon," she says.

"For calling me an asshole?"

"No, you're definitely an asshole, and pretentious and arrogant." She smirks, then the smile fades a little. "I'm sorry for saying no one would ever love you."

I still. My juicy slice of steak suspended on my fork as I gaze at the strange creature who arrived at my house and apologised for the wrong thing. It is the wrong thing. Right?

She interrupts my thoughts. "I want to help you with your research."

"Why?"

"Because I think I could help you, and because there's nothing else to do in this place."

"You have your chores, and once your winter break begins you will need time to type up your work... wouldn't want you to miss your deadline." I make sure to push the point.

"Yes, but what about the rest of the time?" She sighs as if I am obtuse. Irritation tugs at me. She's forgetting her place and her manners. Something will have to be done about that.

Not even a true love's kiss will break that one.

Not that anyone could ever love you.

The words bounce around my head as I chew my steak. I have tried just about every spell and conjuration. Having followed endless rumours of sightings of Eris, I've amassed a useless collection of charms and amulets and still nothing. No change, no cure. Just a collection of failed attempts and broken hopes.

But true love's kiss? It seems impossible to try again, ridiculous. I've failed before.

Once I believed it to be so simple and yet, it has proven the most difficult. How do I get a woman – who I want nothing more than to anger and infuriate so that she gets my body to work again – to love me? She is right. It can't be done, no one can do what needs to be done. No one ever has. Not enough to choose right, not enough to set me truly free. None of them really understood.

I rub my temples as the thoughts churn in my head.

"Fine," I finally say and watch as a smile slices her face.

Maybe the real question is, could I ever love a creature like her?

JINX

I'd hoped that offering to help with his research would have brought about a kind of truce, an exchange where he would want to use my brain over my body. But as soon as Victor takes our dishes away he tells me I'll be reading for him again in the lounge.

My skin crawls as I lean over his chair clutching the papers in my hands, my skirt up, my ass in the air, the heat from the fire warming my pussy. I hate this. And I hate that I am beginning not to hate this even more.

"Read, Jinx," he whispers like a dark suggestion, as if he can't get started till I do, as if my voice somehow commands his movements.

I start, *"The fairy caressed his hard face and returned his smile. "Your father made a wish."*

"My father?"

"Your creator."

"What did he wish for?"

"For you to live."

"That is a great wish. I would like to be alive."

The fairy studied the boy, for he was good and true and naïve; he had only known life for a few fleeting moments, and her smile dimmed.

"Are you not scared to be alive?" His naked palm brushes the cheek of my ass and the words catch in my mouth. I don't know when he peeled away his gloves, his bare hand rough against my exposed ass. His fingers glide down my skin, and gentle as a sigh he slips one over my pussy. I inhale, but there is no air in the room, there is only a monster and he is touching me; *really* touching me. A strangled sound falls from my mouth as he dips two fingers inside me.

"Read," he whispers again as he withdraws his fingers,

and suddenly my lungs flood with air, and I search for words.

I read as his fingers slip back inside me, and this time the sounds come from him, feral and savage.

My voice quivers as words stumble from my mouth and his fingers press in and out of me, and I am mortified to know how very wet I am and how, without even realising, I am shifting myself to his touch.

I stare at the words on the page, they blur as his fingers bury inside me until his knuckles are pressed right up into my body and a thumb begins to circle my clit, pressing, teasing. I almost choke on my gasp.

"Read, Jinx." He sounds menacing, threatening, but I can't find my voice, not when he violates me like this, not when maybe I want him to. The realisation has my throat closing again and a whiny noise drains from my mouth.

I clear it and find my place on the page. I read about the wooden boy and the fairy, the choice she gives him to live or remain a piece of wood forever. I read in broken words and shallow gasps as his fingers dip inside me and tease my clit, building a need that's been dormant for far too long.

The hum between my legs is building into a fever pitch, and I bite off a moan as I ramble off the last few sentences; they sound garbled and swallowed by my breath. It is raspy now and my body feels as if it is on fire and I need relief. His fingers move inside me, and I let the pages fall away, my eyes clenched as tight as my jaw. I'm so close to the apex that is about to wash over me when his fingers vanish and I feel his body move away.

And everything just stops.

Just.

Fucking.

Stops.

"Dorian," I hiss, and it's a mixture of disbelief, anger and disappointment.

I'm greeted only in silence while my nerves feel as though they are all about to snap.

The wood splinters and cracks in the fireplace, blistering the silence that saturates the air between us.

"Why didn't he jump?" he suddenly asks in his raspy voice.

"What?" The fog inside my head clears as I grasp the question. After what he just did to me he is asking about the fucking story?

"The wooden boy, why didn't he jump?"

"Would you?" I grit through clenched teeth, feeling my exposed pussy throb with unanswered need.

"Of course."

I scoff at his easy reply. "No you wouldn't have. You sit here in this house hiding from the world. When was the last time you took a leap?"

"I am not made of wood."

No, you're made of stone. "That doesn't answer the question."

"When was the last time you did?" He turns the question back onto me.

I think about his question. The answer stings the tip of my tongue. "When I agreed to come live with you and let you do... this."

His laughter is cruel and a shiver trembles around my exhausted body. "That wasn't a leap, that was a choice. If I offered to give you all your work back right now, would you stay?"

We both know the answer and so silence shivers between us.

"That's what I thought," he growls as he storms from the room.

DORIAN

My fingers are sticky and I'm torn between sucking them into my mouth for a lingering taste or risk losing her smell that wraps itself around me. I pace my room in a frenzy. It wasn't supposed to feel like that, in fact, it wasn't supposed to feel like anything – nothing has for so fucking long.

It wasn't meant to be about her, but for some godforsaken reason, I was overcome with the need to make her come. I wanted it. So fucking much. I wanted to feel her tight little pussy clench around my fingers and, for a brief moment, I didn't give any fucks about myself or my needs, about my flaccid cock or my gratification. I wanted to see her face twist in agonised pleasure, to know that I was the one responsible for it, the one who dished it out to her. Listening to those sounds falling from her lips; her little whimpers and gasps drove me crazy each time I touched her, almost made me lose my self-control. I almost let it all slip away and be the monster I know I can be. I had to run from her.

But what's more – more important than all of that – is that tonight I became aware of... Something. Jinx maybe hates me, but she doesn't hate it when I touch her. I listened to her little moans and soft gasps, watched her jaw clench and her arms stiffen, watched her body move. She tilted those hips for me and spread herself wider, even if she didn't know she was doing it – I knew. That's not something people can fake.

She was pissed when I withdrew, I knew she was and I diverted well with my questions. Then she ruined it all with her silence.

I grab my chair and smash it on the broken wall. It splinters and the leg hangs limply from the rest of the skeleton. I suck in a long agitated breath. It doesn't matter. None of this matters; it changes nothing at all.

I throw the remains of the chair against the wall. It finally falls to pieces.

15

JINX

"A half-truth is the most cowardly of lies." — Mark Twain

I sit in class listening to Professor Burns talk. His words wash over me as my mind keeps drifting back to Dorian. Even when I'm not with him I'm still his prisoner. I can't get away.

His arrogance and manipulation have cemented themselves under my skin and no matter what I do I can't seem to concentrate. I can't help but re-live what happened after dinner, the way he made me feel, the way his fingers felt inside me, the way my body wanted more.

Heat rushes to my face and I shove the thoughts away, tugging the anger back to the surface. I smirk as I relive the few moments of joy I managed to snatch when calling him an asshole. I hate that I have to cower. I hate that I feel like I have to bite my tongue around him, watch my words, my steps, like any false move could end this for me. That my work could go up in flames in the hearth of his lounge and I will be left with nothing.

I grabbed a quick breakfast before running out of the house, of course not before reading over my 'allowed' schedule for the day. My allowed 'free time' for studies and my allocated time for my chores – those stupid pointless chores, wiping over the same surfaces as if they would become cleaner somehow – then, of course, dinner. Fucking dinner is at six. It's always at six. Despite spending three days at his home I have no idea what he does during the day. I find it hard to believe he remains cooped up in his library the entire time. When I really think about it, I realise I've never seen him leave the house, not even step outside. I guess that's what Victor is for.

Victor. His silence irks me. I know he knows what goes on in that house and yet he hangs around like a shadow. A black ugly stain on the wall that watches silently. A shiver runs up my spine as I wonder how many times he's watched us.

Us. The words quake inside me.

Fucking Dorian and his curse. Maybe I can funnel all my hatred towards curing my host of his shit attitude. Maybe somewhere in his library there is an antidote.

A blur of moving students drags me from my thoughts, and I realise that our class is done and my freedom is coming to its inevitable end. Slinging my backpack over my shoulder, I snake my way around the desks and towards the entrance.

"Miss Hix?"

I stop, draw in a breath, and turn around to find Professor Burns staring at me. "Yes?"

"How is your thesis coming along? You are the only one of my students who hasn't approached me yet."

I swallow. *My thesis is sitting hostage in the hands of a maniac.* "It's fine, in fact, I am heading to the library now to start typing it up."

I look at the clock above his head, watching the time slip away as he blathers on about things that steal away my precious minutes. I nod and hum and keep snatching glances at the time thief that wants my work but won't allow me to complete it.

Eventually, he falls silent.

"Thank you." I'm not even sure if that is the correct response but I turn to walk out of the room.

"Miss Hix." He stops me again. His eyes roam my body, the oversized t-shirt covering my very short skirt. I wish I had a sharp object hiding in my bag. "Are you okay? You seem rather..." his hand gestures in the air in a wave, "off."

"I'm fine thank you, just in a hurry."

His lips thin as he studies me then finally nods, accepting my answer. "Have a good break, I suggest you use your time wisely."

I don't give him any more time as I rush to the library and spend my precious minutes typing away.

||||

The house is quiet when I return, but I am not surprised. Walking to my room I throw my bag on the bed and, following my schedule, go downstairs to complete my chores.

As usual, everything I need waits for me. The hall is deserted, apart from the buckets and cleaning materials left in a pile by the floor, which materialised after I went upstairs.

I sigh and grab the polish expecting another aimless way to spend two hours of my day. It feels like a waste, this routine. Like something you might do with a new puppy when you are trying to train them to behave a certain way. The thoughts crawl inside me like maggots, and I spray the shelf, running the rag over what is normally a smooth polished surface. Instead, the rag catches and snags on the surface.

I stand in front of the sticky shelf, feeling my frustration grow with each passing second. This shelf was pristine when I left this morning – I know because I cleaned it yesterday and the day before. But today, it's coated in a gooey and stubbornly adhesive substance that clings to the wooden surface.

I search the room for signs of him. I know he's there watching. Entertained. I scowl at the emptiness.

I run my fingers over the shelf, they come back gooey and gritty and I fight the urge to smell them. Some things should remain a mystery.

I draw in a long breath, pushing the heavy tangle of nerves into the bottom of my stomach before grabbing the polish and spraying the shelf again. But the stickiness seems to fight back, resisting my attempts to wipe it away and clinging to the rag. The more I scrub the more it feels as if it clings harder. With each swipe of my hand I feel his smirk somewhere growing larger, flaring the anger that embeds itself like a seed inside me.

I throw the useless rag on the ground and try a new tactic, using a scraper to gently chip away at the sticky mess. But even as I make progress, I seem to uncover more and more patches of adhesive substance, hiding just beneath the surface.

My shoulders ache and my hands feel heavy as bit by bit I strip the adhesive off the shelf. It rubs away like my patience, but I can't allow him to win, to see my anger and irritation. I keep my face schooled even as I curse him a thousand times over. If he thought I'd back down and give up, he has another think coming. I shake my head, almost disappointed. He's learned nothing.

Time moves in its unnatural way and though I know my schedule demands two hours, it feels like I have been battling this shelf for a small eternity.

"Your work is done. Dinner is at six." His voice echoes in the large room. I swivel around to look at him, but of course, I can't find him.

I step back and survey my handiwork. The shelf is polished, the sticky residue gone, and a giddy, triumphant sensation filters through me. Fuck him. He can hold my work hostage and play with my body, but he's not going to win any more games.

||||

DORIAN

She falls into her chair; she's not graceful. I can't help but chuckle at her childish antics. Maybe she's still angry. I have no idea why she feels the need to hold onto it. I shrug and wait for Victor to bring out our food. The clock chimes and a moment later our dinner is served.

I dig in, no need for pleasantries. Clearly, this isn't pleasant for either of us. My heart pangs at the thought – I almost wish it was. I shake the feelings away and chew on my lamb, grinding it with my sharp fangs.

Jinx doesn't touch her food, just glares at the fabric that separates us before huffing. "Did you enjoy yourself?"

A smile spreads across my lips as her anger radiates over me. "I have no idea what you're referring to."

I don't bother hiding the amusement in my voice and she huffs out her irritation, mocking me, again. The smile spreads wider across my face. Angry Jinx is my favourite version of her. Her anger makes her animated, powerful and beautiful, and she doesn't even know it.

We eat in silence for a while longer, but as always, Jinx can't stand it. "So, are you going to tell me about this curse?"

I remain silent, chewing slowly and staring at this girl. I want so much to believe that she could be different from the others. I swallow the meat and decide to give her an answer. "I'm the one who's cursed. I thought that would be obvious to you by now."

"Was I right about it? Did it turn you into a righteous asshole?" She has the audacity to smile.

"If you ask my friends they would tell you I was always an asshole."

"If you were always an asshole, do you even have any friends to ask?"

"Touché." There's something entertaining about her quick wit. "I did have friends."

"Did?" Her head tilts and her brow furrows.

I remain silent, taking another bite of my food despite my stomach churning, unease creeping inside me. So much time has passed. Too much.

"Have you ever been in love?" she asks.

I glare at her. I ask her to help me, and suddenly she feels like she can insult me and ask me all these questions. Obviously, I made a mistake.

"Yes, more than once, but even that seems not to be enough," I finally say.

"What do you mean by that?"

I redirect her question. "I had a cat once. I loved it."

"Did it love you?"

I shrug. "It's a fucking animal, what does it know about love?"

"Wow," is all she says. And I have no idea what she means.

"I didn't treat it badly. I fed it and stroked it and let it sleep at the base of my bed."

"It?"

"His name was Maximus Tuna."

She looks at the curtain for a second before she bursts out laughing. "Really?"

"Like a gladiator but with smelly fish," I explain myself for some reason.

Her face changes and a strange look passes over her features.

"What?"

"I just never saw you like that."

"Like what?"

"Being funny."

"It was a long time ago."

"Pity." She shrugs.

I roll my eyes. Is she judging me? Fuck her and fuck her love bullshit. This is the reason it's easier to be with one girl once and never see her again. No feelings, no questions, no mess. Just a good time and they leave.

"Whatever." I huff. "I used to be fun."

"Used to be?"

"Yes."

"But not since your curse?"

I know what she's really asking. She wants me to tell her more. But if I do I might relinquish too much power. The inability to lie is a weakness.

Telling her about my curse and showing her the library was a mistake. I know how to break my curse; she is the one in the dark. Maybe my solution to all this is to keep her occupied long enough, keep her close. Let her chase cold trails and empty leads.

She's still looking at the curtain, waiting for more, and I realise that I've been silent for a while.

"Yes, the curse changed everything." I exhale and slump a little. It feels like a confession. I feel lighter.

She picks up her knife and fork and slices through her meat. Maybe my honesty made her feel a little safer. It's a false feeling, but I need her to start feeling that way around me. I need her to start believing the lie I need to weave around her, without ever saying it out loud. I need her.

"How?" Her eyes grow rounder and she leans in a little as if she knows the enormity of my secret.

"I'm no longer the same man I used to be. The curse... changed me... my appearance..."

"And once you changed?"

"The world around me changed too. My access to things became limited."

"Things?"

"Yes, things." *Rule number one, do not give too many details away, they are easily forgotten. Also, if she knew in this case 'things' meant sinking my dick into women I'm not sure my plan will work.*

She nods and waits for me to continue.

"I could no longer live the same lifestyle or enjoy the same benefits once this change occurred."

"What was your lifestyle?"

"That's not important." *Rule number two. Omit specifics, without details you can remain hidden.*

"I see," she says, and I see the edge of her mouth tighten and her jaw clench ever so slightly. She's masking her irritation or perhaps swallowing down her curiosity, saving her questions for another time.

Either way that's all she's going to get.

Her eyes narrow trying to see beyond the curtain that separates us. I can tell she's unsatisfied, but instead of asking more questions she knows she'll not get answers to, she rolls her shoulders back, straightening her back.

"How can I help?"

I watch her chewing, her lips glistening. "You will have access to my library, but there will be rules."

"Shocker," she mumbles under her breath but the words carry over to me. My lips twitch in an unexpected smile.

"You must always knock before entering. I need to be... Prepared."

She nods as I list my demands, swallowing them down with her food.

"When can we get started?" she asks when I'm done.

"After you read to me tonight."

"Can we skip reading today?"

"Why? You do not want your pages?"

"Of course I do, but maybe we can skip it and work in the library instead."

"That was not the deal."

"Deals are negotiable."

"Not this one. You will read to me. Our time in the library is how you choose to use your free time. If you decide to skip our reading session you will forfeit your pages. You have ten seconds to decide."

"What? Wait."

"Eight.... Seven." I count down watching the panic settle around her features.

"I'll read," she mumbles and pushes away from the table, her meal only half-eaten.

"Good girl," I whisper in her wake, taking my time before I get to the lounge.

She's already there, already bent over for me, already ripe and glistening and beautiful. It's why I don't dare touch her tonight. "Read."

DORIAN

J inx is tucked in her bed, sleeping peacefully for a change, while I stand in the rose garden, the sweet smell almost dizzying. I brood about the past. Our dinner conversation dredged up too many memories.

In the first weeks I became obsessed with my reflection, but as the changes appeared and grew more apparent, more brutal, more severe, I could no longer stand the sight of myself. Every mirror has been broken and shut away, as I felt each one of my lies engraved on my face, carved with broken bones into my body and sealed with a terrifying look – my reflection only sent a hollow wretched feeling inside me – sickening me to my core.

When the curse had completely taken over, I had shunned myself away in the first few years, never leaving the west wing, let alone the house. Maybe it's why I now spend most of my nights outside, why I detest being inside. The fear that had consumed me stole so much of my time, so many wasted years. They don't really matter. The curse seems to have made everything timeless. Time stretches around me eerily, surreal.

I have felt remorseful, on more than one occasion, crying and howling into the dark night, screaming at the moon and cursing the universe, and with each failed attempt, with each broken promise I grew more desperate, more angry and I never knew if my remorse was for my deeds or perhaps for choosing Eris that night. For if I had not been caught, none of this would have happened.

But perhaps the most pathetic of it all was that I did hide. The fear of being seen or maybe even hunted, tormented me, stalked me like a menacing shadow. But it was for naught. No one came looking. Not for me. My manager wanted his salary and stockholders wanted their cuts, but no one was looking for *me*. I was forgotten the moment I was out of sight. And it turned out I wasn't unique enough, pretty enough, special enough. Just like everyone else, I was disposable.

Until one day Victor found me.

A lost traveller, he thought he'd found a beast worth killing, worth exposing, worth exploiting. But what he didn't realise was how strong I was, how brutal the loneliness had made me, how cold, how heartless. I imprisoned him that night. The basement became his home, with meagre food or water. I was unused to company and keeping him fed and watered was not my concern, only I was. My needs had to be met, the curse had to be broken, deals had to be brokered and consequences dealt with. It was the desperation that had truly transformed me.

He became a witness to all my horror and I punished him with my deeds, forcing him to do the worst, stealing his humanity day by day, till he was just as beastly as I was. He swore that if I'd let him go he would never tell a soul, would never betray me. But of course I couldn't trust him. I knew he would return with an army and take me away, punish me for all the cruelty I had put him through.

He begged and begged till I cut out his tongue to silence him. I swore to him that I would never let him go, I would let him rot in my basement watching my shame, feasting on my horror till he took his last breath. That night I made him watch as I ate his cut-up tongue. That was the first time I had seen a grown man cry. I remember thinking it was the most pathetic sight I had ever seen in my life, but that was before the desperation took hold of me and strangled every last drop of hope I had left. Before I was totally broken. Before I crumpled beneath the weight of it all and wept like a guilty addict, remembering a time when life was the way it was meant to be.

In the end we both became prisoners, and when enough time had passed, he was just as broken as I was. By consuming part of him and shrouding him in my curse, I somehow bound him to me. Like me, he did not age, did not feel the fingers of time clawing at him – ushering him to his grave. Maybe it was the loneliness we both felt that drew us closer, that made me spend endless, needless hours with him, that in time allowed me to release his chains. But none of it mattered any longer – we were bound together, and like me, he only has one way out.

I see the way he looks at her; there's a hunger there, a desperate need. She's *his* final hope.

I smell the roses, their perfume reminds me of the past... but maybe, just maybe Jinx can be our future.

||||

We while away the afternoons of the next few days. With her in my space, I find time moves differently. She keeps surprising me. More intelligent than I would have given someone like her credit for, her questions are no longer personal but perceptive and keen. She's digging, searching, interested. She's fast falling into a bottomless dark hole into which I pushed her, knowing full well there are no answers at the bottom because there is no bottom.

Where my struggle lies is with the idle chit-chat, the

random empty conversations people have to fill silences. I've never spent this much time with another person. I've never had to fill up their emptiness, and I find it both intimidating and fascinating. The way she seems interested in the most mundane of details. She applies her interest equally to her research and to studying me. And the more interest she shows, the more drawn I am to this odd girl. I find that being around her makes everything inside me buzz and hum, like a rusty machine that's been oiled – all the parts begin to move and ache and scream.

It's a good kind of pain. It reminds me that I'm alive.

I like watching her, the way her hips move when she glides around the library and how her lips move when she reads to herself. The way her skin pinks when it's under the hot water in her shower and the way her hair falls across her face when she sleeps.

I study her in much the same way she studies my books. Learning every small and intimate detail, and it seems we've only just begun.

16

DORIAN

"The truth is messy. It's raw and uncomfortable. You can't blame people for preferring lies." — Holly Black, Red Glove

"So you definitely can't shapeshift?"

"No, it's not that kind of curse." I sigh, exasperated.

"Well, I guess therianthropy is out." She closes the book and sets it aside.

"Yes, but I already told you that," I snap, unsure why. It was my idea to lead her astray to begin with and now that she is so far off the mark, I find myself agitated.

She ignores my tantrum and rolls her eyes. "I already told you that," she mimics in a childish tone. "Sometimes it's good to have a second pair of eyes go over things."

"Fine."

"Why are you angry with me?"

"I'm not angry with you."

"You have a funny way of showing it."

My scalp itches again and I squeeze my fists by my sides to stop myself from pulling off the uncomfortable veil over my head and scratching till I bleed.

"I'm not angry, I'm frustrated."

"With me?"

I don't answer. What good will that do? She looks at me for a few seconds and the fire in her eyes seems to dim.

"Can I get the rest of my pages back?"

I cross my arms over my chest and glare at her, of course, she can't tell. "I have given you what you've earned."

Her eyes fall away from me and onto her hands, her fingers twisted together in a strange knot.

I grind my teeth. *Fuck*, I've somehow made things worse. Why do I care so much? I suck in a quick breath and try to derail her train of thought.

"I'm not frustrated with *you*."

"What then?"

I grind my teeth again. *What does she think?* "Everything."

At that, she steps closer to me and her eyes narrow, scrutinising me behind the veil, searching for something. Whatever she thinks she finds makes her reach for my gloved hand, and I still.

"Tell me about your curse." Her voice is so soft, so kind, so caring, my insides convulse with a new unexpected feeling I cannot yet place. It's both comforting and terrifying.

I pull my hand away but don't move.

"It was a woman, she cursed me."

"Was she an ex?"

I snort, then cover up with a cough when she frowns. "I've never really 'dated'."

"Why?"

I shrug, how could I even begin to explain? "Dating felt like too much hard work."

"Hard work?"

"Sure, girls want to be taken to fancy restaurants and be wooed, they want chocolates and flowers and jewellery. It just wasn't my thing."

She shakes her head, and I swear I see pity painting her face.

"What?" I ask as agitation prickles my skin. How fucking dare she pity me? Me?

"That's not what girls want."

"Sure it is."

"If you say so, you're obviously an expert."

I don't miss her sarcasm, but her words baffle me. Of course it's what they want. It's what they wanted from *me*. Fancy dinners at stupid expensive restaurants, jewels and ridiculously expensive clothes, they wanted my vast financial wealth as well as my cock. They all wanted *that*. But not a single one of them wanted anything more.

"Prove me wrong then, what do they want?"

"Connection." She says it as if it is the most obvious thing in the world. "They want to be seen for who they are, not a composite of a picture of what other people think they should be."

"Connection?"

"Sure, that's why people date. It's not about the fancy dinners and flowers, it's doing something you both enjoy and getting to know one another."

"What do you enjoy doing?" I blurt it out feeling stupid.

"On a date?"

I shrug.

"Lots of things."

"Like?"

"A cup of coffee in a small cafe, a walk in the park, watching a movie, watching the sunset."

"Those feel... Simple."

"They should."

"So you never want to go to fancy restaurants?"

"I didn't say that, everyone likes to be spoiled from time to time, but I'd much rather take a walk and share a few laughs getting to know someone than sit in some stuffy restaurant, and have to shout over the rest of the diners and wonder if the guy across from me is overcompensating for something."

I don't miss her smirk and I'm finding it hard to believe her. Women crave wealth, not simplicity.

"And if he wants to show off his wealth by taking her there and is not overcompensating for anything?"

"Then he might never know if she came on that second date for his personality or his money."

I tilt my head and stare at her. It can't be that simple. "Would you like to watch the sunset with me?"

Her head jerks up and I think I see her grimace before she recovers. "You like sunsets?"

"Doesn't everyone?"

"I guess."

"Great, tomorrow after dinner then." I'm suddenly excited and I'm not even sure why.

"Can I get the rest of my pages?"

Her question jars me. Why is she back on the pages when she's just agreed to go on a date with me?

"Soon."

"When?"

"Do you want to leave?"

She casts her eyes down and nods. "I need to get home."

"Why? What do you have out there?"

"I don't know, but I won't find out being locked up in here..." Her eyes glisten when she looks up again, "I need to get home."

"You're not my prisoner, you can leave anytime you

want." Even as the words spill out of my mouth I try to catch them and shove them back inside. But the trickle begins and soon it will be a waterfall of pain.

"We both know that's a lie."

Fuck.

Her whiny voice is nothing but a dim ring over the harsh hum that thrums in my skull. My heart kicks out, beating so fast I hope it might shatter and end this, instead, the first tingle of pins jabs my skin.

"Get out," I bark, my voice harsh and feral.

"What are yo—"

"Get out!" I scream as my bones begin to vibrate. Jinx stares at me, confusion and anger mars her face, but she doesn't leave.

In a desperate move, I grab her by the elbow, drag her towards the door and shove her. It's not gentle, and her small body flies out of the library. Her head collides with the wall on the opposite side. She shrieks, maybe in pain, maybe in fear, but it doesn't really matter, not as the pain begins to erase everything around me.

I slam the door shut in her wake. The excruciating pain is so familiar, though I haven't felt it in so long. I hear the first crack and scream then fall to my knees as bones shatter in my back and push their way under my skin, rearranging, shifting, like drifting continents.

Now that she is safely out of the room I let my body succumb to the pain and shriek in agony.

||||

JINX

M y head throbs where it hit the wall. A rush of pain echoes inside me. Feral screams emanate from behind the closed door, more animal than human.

Fear crackles through me as I rush towards the front door and towards my car, not looking back.

Pain resonates inside my skull with each step as if my face is getting pounded over and over again. I can feel the skin swell around my eye and feel hot liquid spill down my cheek. I don't stop to check if it's blood or tears. My vision blurs, my feet kicking up mud that plasters itself to my legs.

I run blindly. My feet splash in puddles, my heart rumbles like the threatening sky above. I stumble, throwing my hands out, and collide with the hard shell of my cold car, stopping my fall.

I no longer think, no longer care. He is a monster, and he can keep my pages, my words, my life in his demented hands. I have to get away, far away from him, from this place.

I start my engine and large drops begin to splash on my windscreen as the sky opens up in a deluge. My tyres spin in the mud as I drive away.

||||

M y apartment feels smaller. It's only been a week and yet the place feels abandoned.

Slamming the door behind me, I head straight to the bathroom and look at my reflection. A streak of blood has congealed along my cheek and down to my jawline. I touch my swollen face and wince. That's going to hurt more in the morning.

I feel dirty. The oversized T-shirt Dorian has given me

hangs loosely over my mud-streaked legs and my body feels tired, drained.

I grab the hem of the shirt, wanting to rip it from my body and wash away the memories of the last few days when I hear the banging at my door.

"Open up." His voice sends a slither of panic along my body.

He keeps pounding at my door. Dragging myself to the small lounge room, I stare at the door, watching it shiver as his fists pound on the other side. "Jinx!"

"Go away," I choke out, fear and froth clogging my throat.

"Open this door now!"

My feet won't listen to the rest of me as they drag me forward towards the door and my hands wrap around the cold knob. If I don't open it he will just keep pounding and the neighbours will peek out of their homes and there will be a complaint. I can't lose this place too, not with being late with the rent, again.

I unlock the door and step back as it flies open. He stands there, his body covered in his stupid veil and over-sized clothes as it heaves. Behind him I find Victor. His gaze runs along my face as my lungs fight for air. His face remains stoic.

"What took you so long?" Dorian's harsh growl cleaves the silence and fills the room with a cold chill. He steps forward, cupping my chin and forcing me to look at him..

"Let me go," I hiss as his long fingers dig into my skin.

"You left, that is against the rules."

"You hurt me." I try to step out of his clutch, but he grips me tighter.

"That was an accident."

"That's not an apology."

Behind his veil, his head shifts as if he is taking in the room. "This place is... small."

I say nothing as tears pool in my eyes and his fingers claw at my skin. The pain in my head slithers down my neck.

Dorian releases my face and takes my hand. It's strong beneath the velvety glove that hides it. My legs lock, unable to move. I feel the weight of his stare on me a second before he lifts me in a swift move and carries me to the breakfast bar, placing me on top. I feel tiny in his arms.

"Watch her," he grinds out at Victor who stands at my door, a dark expression clouding his face.

Dorian walks around my apartment, opening cupboards. When he comes back he has a glass of water, two pills, cotton balls and a bottle of antiseptic.

He hands me the water and puts the pills in my hand. "Drink." He waits, impatience radiating off him as I swallow the pills and empty the glass.

He steps closer again, tucking himself in between my legs, his wide body inches from mine. Up here we are almost the same height. My gaze falls away from his veil-covered face. I want to get away from him. He reaches over to the cotton ball and antiseptic before he cups my chin again. It's gentler this time, as he swipes at my temple and along my cheek. Slow, tender wipes that burn and sting. I suck in a sharp breath as the cold liquid bites at my skin, and my heart skitters at his touch. His gentle caress is a strange unfamiliar contradiction to his cold harshness.

When he's done, he sets the cotton ball down but doesn't move. I can feel the heat radiate from his body and his face inches closer to mine. "Thank you," I whisper, and he nods, his fingers tracing my wound.

I wince at the touch and his fingers feather my cheek

and along my jaw. I suck in a sharp breath and he abruptly steps back and away.

"It's time to go home."

"I am home," I whisper.

"This isn't your home until our deal is complete."

When I remain silent, his head tilts, and I wonder what he sees when he looks at me. He can cover himself all he wants, all I see is a monster.

"Are you ready to go?"

No. Of course I am not ready, I have just escaped his lair and like a shadow, he's followed me into my sanctuary, invaded my space. But the way his fingers caressed my skin, the way he was so very gentle, his close, terrifying proximity almost makes me feel safe.

Almost.

Bryan chooses that moment to appear at my door. I wonder what he must think as he sees the silent giant no more than two steps inside my apartment, and me on the kitchen island, hovered over by a hulking man covered from head to toe in clothes and a veil that shields his face from the world. He freezes as his gaze sweeps over the scene and lands on my swollen eye.

"What's going on here?" He tries to sound brave but Bryan isn't brave, he is a smarmy little worm who makes me feel dirty every time he gives me his grimy little smile like he's looking under my clothes.

"Who is that?" Dorian doesn't pay him any attention, as if giving him any is a total waste of his time.

"My landlord."

"What does he want?" he asks me.

"Her rent is due," Bryan answers for me. I feel the heat of Dorian's breath as he sighs long and hard.

"What does he want?" he asks again as if he didn't hear Bryan speak at all.

"She owes me three months' worth of—" Bryan starts again, but Victor turns to him, giving him a long hard look. Bryan takes a step backwards, I don't even know if he realises he's done it.

"He wants his rent."

"Are you behind?"

"Yes." My eyes fall away from the monster who is calm and subdued before me.

"I thought you said your work pays your bills."

"It does, just not all of them on time."

"What will he do if you don't have it?"

"He'll offer me an extension if I suck his cock."

Somewhere behind Victor, I hear Bryan start to protest before he is shut down. A cold chill passes between us, and all of Dorian's muscles stiffen.

"And have you?"

Anger creeps inside me as bile claws at my throat. What I do to survive is none of his business, not that I would ever stoop so low as to touch that slimy freak anyway. "Fuck no."

"I see." Despite the veil that covers his face, I can feel the intensity of his glare on my face.. Fuck him, I don't owe him any explanations.

"My new employer is due to pay me Wednesday, I'll be fine." I jab at him.

"Wednesday is a long way away." His sharp voice shuts me up. I feel like a school kid at the principal's office. "Are you ready to go home now?" he asks again, and this time it no longer feels like a question.

"Yes." I throw my head up and look at the ceiling, wincing at the pain in my eye. He knows all the ways to hurt me.

"Good." He turns to Victor. "Take her to the car and wait for me. Bryan and I have some business to discuss."

"Wait."

"What now?" His agitation swarms around me.

"I just want some clothes."

His inhale is sharp and impatient. "You have two minutes."

I know there's no arguing with him and a clock is ticking down in his head. I jump off the counter and rush to my room, grabbing a bag and stuffing whatever clothes I find into it.

It doesn't feel like enough time before Victor shows up, slinging my bag over his shoulder and then, as if I were a child, carries me out of my apartment and towards the stairwell, kicking the door closed behind us.

Despite myself, I find my arms clutching his strong shoulders and nuzzling into his chest. There's something about his smell, his warmth, his silence, that lets me know I'll be okay. But just as the thought drifts inside me I hear the screams. They rush from beneath my closed apartment door and follow us all the way to the car till Victor settles me in the back seat and closes the door, silencing the world.

He slams his own door as he settles in his seat, and I turn my attention to him.

"What's he doing to him?"

Victor says nothing, of course. I shake my head and stare at the darkening sky through the tinted windows and wait, a few droplets of rain hit the window in violent slashes.

A few moments later, Dorian opens the door and slides in beside me. "Take us home."

Victor starts the engine and we pull away from my apartment complex.

"What did you do to Bryan?"

"Tell me, Jinx," he continues as if he didn't hear my question at all, "if Bryan looked different, taller perhaps, handsome, would you have gotten on your knees to suck his cock?"

"Of course not!" I huff out.

"Are you sure?"

Am I? If he was handsome and well-kempt would I have any problems selling my dignity for a little bit of time? "Yes." We both hear the uncertainty in my voice.

Dorian scoffs and irritation skittles across my skin.

"Did *you* offer him a blow job?" I throw at him.

"No."

"Would you have given him a blow job if he looked differently? If he was charming and good-looking?" I feign bravery and push on.

Dorian's head swivels sharply towards mine and all the sarcasm drains from my face. "No."

I gulp down the fear that settles in my throat. "What did you do then?"

"I offered him a choice."

"So why was he screaming?"

"He chose wrong," is all he says and remains silent for the rest of our drive back.

17

JINX

"Even the truth is just a mere thought." — Mokokoma Mokhonoana

The monster closes in, I feel it, it brings with it darkness and shadows and they consume me, there's no way out. I scream.

I wake up to a silent room and catch my breath. My bed is empty, but when I look around, I realise I'm not alone. Dorian stands over my bed, his broad body looming over me. I shoot up and scoot backwards till I hit the headboard. Grabbing the sheet, I clutch it to my chest, like it could protect me from his invasion. A bead of sweat rolls down my cheek, I swipe at it and wince at the swollen flesh. Anger drips inside me.

"What the hell are you doing in my room?" My eyes swing around, searching. For a way out? I'm not sure.

"It's dinner time."

"So?"

"You were sleeping, and I didn't think you'd want to miss it."

"You could have knocked."

"I did." He sounds genuine.

I glare at him for a minute. I didn't sleep well last night. My only consolation is that winter break is upon me and I won't have to explain my appearance to anyone. Still, his temper scares me enough that I've stayed holed up in the room. I didn't do his chores or go down to the library. I must have succumbed to the boredom and tiredness and fell asleep again.

"I'll see you downstairs."

He turns to leave without looking back, and I stay rooted to the bed, the echo of my dream beating inside me as he closes the door behind him. When I'm certain he's gone I climb out of bed. To my right I find an open suitcase with a selection of brand new clothes – none of them mine – as I go through them, I find they are all short, tight and reveal-ing. I clench my fists, the nails digging into my palm. I know I could spend a day looking for the bag of clothes he'd allowed me to pack earlier, and I know I'll never find them. I let out a sharp exhale. At least I don't have to wear his stupid boxers anymore.

I find a long-sleeved shirt, a short skirt and some lacy underwear – all black, all tight, all perfectly suited to my figure. I feel comfort in the long sleeves like they give me a place to hide.

Dinner is a strange and uncomfortable ordeal. An orchestra of clinking cutlery and long silences. Victor clears up our dishes and exits the room. I stand to leave when Dorian's voice slices through the lull.

"Where are you going?"

"To my room."

"But we have a date." He sounds wounded. "Have you forgotten?"

"I'm not going on a date with you, Dorian, you hurt me."

"That was an accident." He pulls the veil aside and suddenly he is beside me, his broad body hulking above me. "I've already told you that." He reaches out as if to touch me then jerks his hand away remembering himself.

"You still haven't apologised." I glare at him.

"I got you some new clothes."

I roll my eyes. This man is unbelievable. "That's not an apology. And I liked my clothes, they were mine and they were comfortable."

"These are new."

"But they aren't mine."

"They are now."

I huff and roll my eyes; he doesn't understand anything.

Silence falls between us like frozen sleet.

"I'm sorry," he says in a gentle voice that I've not heard him use before.

Even behind his mask and gloves and bulky suit, I feel his vulnerability, something about him that screams for help. Behind all that anger and hatred there is a man so broken he has vanquished himself to this sad, isolated house away from society and people. Somewhere he can hide. Maybe not just himself but his pain. But today, despite all that, he left it – for me. He leapt. And maybe I need to leap too.

I sigh and reach for him. He freezes. A twisted sculpture bent out of shape. I slide my hand around his arm, noticing his shoulders stiffen and his muscles tense. "Come on. You promised me a sunset."

We stand for a few more seconds as if he is completely lost inside himself before he regains control. Ease slides back into his body as he relaxes and calls Victor.

"The car, quick, we don't have much time." Thunder rolls across the sky as if punctuating his words."

||||

JINX

I leave the house for a second time that day, but this time I am not alone and I am not running from something but hurtling towards something else altogether. Victor manoeuvres the car expertly over the slick road that meanders towards the mountains that usually keep the house in shadow. He is chasing the sun and the faster we go, the quicker it leaves us behind.

We climb to the top of the smaller of the two hills that loom over the house and he parks in a driveway of yet another abandoned property. This one feels unlived-in but that if it were, it would be inhabited by royalty.

Medieval in style, the place seems to have been cut out of a fairy tale book and stuck here on this mountain. Looking up at the imposing rock threaded by years of growing creepers and vines, I half wonder if a princess might have once been locked up in the highest tower, but I have no time to dwell on the beauty and the wonder of this place as Dorian grabs my wrist and leads me inside.

We are greeted by the echoing clap of pigeon wings as they take off in the deserted stone chambers, and the sun's rays, which streak from broken windows, paint the floor and desolate walls a kaleidoscope of scarlets and tangerines.

"This way." He keeps dragging me away.

"What is this place?"

"A memory."

Before I have a chance to ask what he means he pulls me out of the main house and onto a balcony. The sight takes my breath away. The wide balcony has been extended out over a rock face, jagged greys and clouded ashen stone rise sheer from the valley below. The deck is set with a table, deck chairs and champagne flutes. On the table a sweating bottle awaits.

I edge to the ledge, peering beneath me, finding a sheer drop that seems endless. "Careful, if you stare too long into the abyss, the abyss begins to stare back at you." His words splinter my thoughts and send a shiver along my skin. I spin to find him by the small table.

"Would you like a drink?"

I blink a few times, then nod. "Sure."

He advances with a flute of champagne, and I take the drink from him before peering once again over the precipice.

"It's incredible how something so beautiful can be so scary."

"Indeed," he replies, and all I feel is the weight of his gaze from behind the veil that shields him from me.

I take a long sip of the champagne, the bubbles dancing their way down my throat and I chance another quick look over the cliff face. The setting sun falling beyond the horizon takes away the last warm tendrils of the day. "Where's Victor?" A safe topic.

"He's probably waiting in the car." Dorian comes to stand by me and peers over the edge.

"Was he military? You know, before he worked for you?"

"You should ask him," he snaps back, and I feel like I've upset him.

"You are awfully cruel to him."

"Am I?"

136

"You are; it's probably why he never says a thing."

He moves a little. "He's a mute."

"So he can't talk?"

He sighs, as if I am that child again stating the obvious. "Just because he can't talk doesn't mean he can't communicate. Maybe it's you who's being cruel."

I ponder his words and think about the short interactions I've had with Victor. The way his face twists and his eyes narrow and his head dips when he looks at me. Maybe I wasn't paying enough attention. "You're right."

"Of course I am."

"And so humble."

"Well..." He shrugs. "It takes a lot of work to be this perfect."

"You think of yourself as perfect?"

He goes quiet for a moment. "I used to think I was."

"And what was that like?"

"Satisfying. It made me greedy."

"How so?" I turn to look at him as he leans against the balcony. I feel his eyes on me, tracing my face from behind the veil.

"Beauty and perfection is much like your cliff here; it gives people something to look at while filling them with a false sense of security. They trust more easily, give more freely." He stops for a moment. "But beauty is a dangerous lie, the more they give the more you want."

"Why?"

"Because it's fun."

"Is that it?" I quirk an eyebrow.

He thinks for a moment before he answers. "No."

"Then why?"

"Because the more they give, the emptier you feel." There is something so broken about his voice that makes me want to wrap myself around him and protect him from the world. I take a tentative step towards him then stop. If I'm protecting the monster, who is going to protect me?

I let his words churn through me. "Why did you keep taking then?"

"What else was there to do?"

"Give?"

"I've tried that before."

"And didn't it make you feel good?"

He shakes his head. "No, it was a lie."

"I don't understand."

"The sun is setting." He tries to turn my attention away.

"What was the lie?"

"You're going to miss it," he says as I keep leaning against the banister, my back to the sunset.

"What did you give?"

In a swift move, Dorian comes to stand in front of me and grabs my hands, spinning me around. My breath lurches out of my lungs as he pins me against the banister with his body and cages me with his arms, one on each side of me.

The sky is burning. Orange and gold stretches far and wide as the sun dips beyond the horizon beckoning twilight. It's beautiful. My heart thrums as I feel Dorian's body against mine. Hard and jagged like the rocks, and I wonder if he is just as beautiful. I'm already sure he is just as dangerous.

I'm trapped in his arms and the rapture of the sunset, the orange ball of fire sinking quickly beneath the sea. Dorian's body moves with the sun and I feel it sliding down against mine, just enough till his mouth is by my ear.

"My soul," he whispers, and the heat of his breath fans my ear. I shiver at the words as he releases me.

When I turn to him, he is walking back into the house and I am breathless.

I watch him walk away and try to consolidate the monster and the broken man who hides inside it. Dorian is like an ocean, ever-changing, angry and petulant and other times gentle and calm. I want to see more of him.

"Dorian, wait," I call after him as tendrils of night slither across the sky and curtain us in darkness. He stops, waits but doesn't turn around. I start walking towards him. "Tell me about that, about giving your soul away. What does that mean?"

In the fading light, I see his shoulders stiffen and his head tilt. "No." His tone sends a cold chill inside me.

I stop dead in my tracks. He turns then, and inhales, letting out a long drawn out-breath.

"I really am sorry for hurting you." I feel his intense stare. "Good night, Jinx, thank you for a lovely time. Victor will take you home." He does a strange bow as if unsure how to end the conversation, then walks into the dark cavernous house, leaving me wrapped in darkness and engulfed in confusion.

||||

DORIAN

My heart still throbs even three hours later, like it's been sliced open and a fly has somehow embedded itself inside the troublesome organ. It feels almost alive. I almost allowed it to spill its greatest secret and the admission felt so raw and delicate and fragile and *good*. It gave me an odd sense of joy. And yet I could not give her the truth, not everything she asked for.

The walk back helped me clear my head, remember my purpose, my need. Visiting the castle after so many years reminded me of all the paths that led me here. I only bought it when I heard it belonged to Eris. A desperate, broken part of me believed it. Back then when things were fresh and the pain searing, I would have believed anything. It was a time that hope still meant something and opportunity wasn't anything I could let go.

I'd spent years cooped up in the castle, sitting in its empty stone chambers, shivering in the darkness, waiting for her to return. Staring at that cold stone face tiled beautifully into the floor. But just like me, it was abandoned and left to rot away. Only in a certain light at the right time of day when you caught a glimpse you could tell it was once beautiful. I bought the house below and carved out the mosaic of her face, placing it instead at my feet, like it should have always been and then I sat in wait. I still sit and wait, but I realised long ago she will never return.

I shake away the memories as I watch Jinx stretch on the bed, a book in her hands. Her eyes scan the pages, and her teeth pull in her plump lower lip.

Her presence dredges up more of the past. It's probably because I can't help comparing how different she is to the others. *The others.* They all wanted their cash and all stared in horror at my broken face and gnarled body. The few who managed to get past the initial disgust, barely allowed me to touch them, their bodies stiffening like corpses at my barely-there brush of their skin. Whimpers bled from their lips and their eyes clenched closed, too afraid to look at the monster that needed to be touched, that wanted to fuck them, that needed to feel.

But it was all empty and hollow, their reactions to me kept my body broken and my cock flaccid till the hope was drained along with my beauty and I became the empty monster she cursed me to be.

I draw in a long breath refusing to feel sorry for myself. Those days are over, a far away buried past that I refuse to revisit. And yet with every beat of my frazzled heart hope pumps through my body, like Jinx has injected it into my veins. I know I am keeping her here against her will, but then, every now and again there is something there, something that keeps her here – it's more than fear, it's more than hatred, it's more than the need to collect her words. I try not to think about it. I step away from the peephole and creep into the darkness of my room trying to push away the word, keep it out in the emptiness, but still it follows me into the shadows and buries itself like a worm.

18

JINX

"The truth is rarely pure and never simple." — Oscar Wilde

I wake up to a room saturated in bright sunlight. The wooden panels, shaded yellow and white, radiating heat like a low-burning furnace. It feels like a Sunday, like a weekend morning where all responsibilities have been shed and life feels a little less stressful and full. Of course it's not, and as I yawn I wince at the pain in my face and tentatively brush over the swollen skin.

A small shudder passes inside me. After my 'date' with Dorian, I feel a little lighter, like maybe this house isn't so full of monsters but scared men who don't know how to face their demons. I feel giddy. I don't know why; maybe the realisation that a human lives behind the veil makes me feel safe at last.

I leave the bed and make my way to the bathroom where I splash some water on my face before studying it in the mirror. My eye is swollen. A dark purple ring stains my skin and each minute movement of my face sends a slight sliver of pain to my eye. Like a constant reminder of what's happened, of what he is capable of. I sigh and try to remember the other side of my captor, the one that's slightly less dark and violent but rather more tender and caring.

I make it halfway to the kitchen before I see Dorian. He leans against the door of the library.

"Good morning." I'm bouncing on the balls of my feet.

"Good morning." He sounds surprised. "It's still early."

"I know."

"Your duties don't start till later." I feel him frown, it's heavy and sharp, but I refuse to let the feeling drag me down today.

"I know, but thank you so much for explaining it to me." I feel braver now as I feel his gaze on my face.

If my rebuke irks him he gives nothing away. "Well then, are you going to join me?"

"No. I'm going to explore your garden and relax. You should try it sometime."

"Relaxing?"

"Yes."

"But the research—"

"Can wait another day, or you can go on without me." I don't wait for an answer, I simply walk into the kitchen where I grab some fruit and biscuits, throw them into a plastic container and walk out the door feeling his eyes on me.

I walk around the house, the long wooden porch creaking beneath my feet before I step off at the back. There is something in the air, everything feels magical, almost perfect as I walk into the manicured garden watched over by the two mountain peaks now bathed in sun. The green grass sways gently in the breeze as if it was a green sea. I tilt my head towards the sun, feeling the gentle warmth, noticing how the sky is a darker blue the higher my eyes wander. The gentle rays permeate my skin when movement catches my eye.

Victor appears from somewhere in the garden, his torso naked and covered in sweat, his mud-covered hands carrying a shovel and fresh roses. He freezes when he sees me. He stands, stoic and unflinching. His eyes track my face and rake down my body before meeting my eyes once more.

"Sorry," I mumble, as he keeps staring at me. "I didn't mean to interrupt."

"Don't mind him." Dorian's voice slithers behind me, and I jump, feeling my heart in my throat. I spin to find him standing behind me. "He was just tending to the rose garden. He's done now."

Victor nods and brushes by us as he makes his way back into the house.

"The roses take much work to keep alive in this weather."

I stare at Dorian. His sudden appearance has rattled me.

"Let me show you around."

He steps farther into the garden and like a sheep, I follow him. The air is pungent with the fragrance of jasmine and roses as we cut through the vast garden that seems to expand forever. I have only seen gardens like this in pictures. They usually belong to the rich with copious leisure time and money, and once again I find myself wondering more and more about my mysterious host and his background.

We walk in silence, exploring the garden, the various plants and flowers that bloom from the mud-drenched earth until we reach a small body of water. It is not a natural basin, but an artificial addition. Shallow waves lap at the scattered round pebbles that frame it.

I step closer to the edge and crouch down. From five feet

up, the surface is an opaque green, but from just two it's clear enough to see the plants and life below the surface. Flashes of scaly tales and seaweed dance and mingle below the surface.

"It's beautiful," I whisper more to myself than to him as I inhale slowly. This place is so peaceful.

"Would you like to catch one?"

"One what?"

"A fish." He exhales in the way that he does when he feels as if he is talking to a petulant child.

"I've never—"

"I'll teach you," he cuts me off and walks away to a small shed I notice for the first time. The door whines like an old lady and Dorian comes back a few seconds later carrying a fishing rod and a small jar. When he sets it down, I see it is alive with wiggling maggots, and bile rises up my throat.

Dorian reaches into the jar and grabs a maggot before hooking it on the end of the line. He casts his fishing line. His back shifts and strains as his arms curve in an arch before the line hits the water. I follow his gaze, watching the line in the water as it bobs beneath the surface. When I turn back to him his face is turned towards me. I shudder under it.

He reels his line and gets ready to cast again. I watch in fascination as his body becomes one with the rod, all one singular focused being in a perfect gentle dance, until it hits the water and the fluidity falls away from him and he becomes like the rock.

"Do you ever catch anything?"

"Every time." There is something about the way he says it that makes me shiver, despite the hot sun burning above us. "Your turn." His dark voice grows suddenly softer and he gestures for me to come to him.

I wait until he reels in his line. I stand beside him and he passes me the rod. It's surprisingly light. The bamboo is slick and smooth against my palm and bends slightly at the top as I wiggle it. Dorian places a hand on my shoulder and gives it a slight squeeze. It's enough for me to understand his disapproval and I stop. He obviously takes his fishing very seriously. Like everything else.

"What do I do now?"

"Hold and cast."

The water suddenly seems too far away despite it only being a few feet from where we're standing. I grip the rod and close my eyes thinking of the way Dorian moved, the way his hands arched and his body leaned as if he was an extension of the line. I open my eyes and throw my hands out wildly. The line shoots out but falls short of the water.

I huff.

"Again."

When I do, I fail for a second then a third and fourth time. After my fifth attempt I shove the rod back in his face. "This is stupid. I can't do this."

I know he is staring at me from behind his veil, frozen. For a few moments, he says nothing, just shakes his head. "Again."

"No." I shove it back at him and still he refuses to take it. He grunts an irritated sound. "I said try again."

"I said I don't want to." When he doesn't take the rod I simply let it fall out of my hands and start walking away.

With unexpected reflexes Dorian catches the rod in one hand and grabs onto my arm with the other. He pulls me forcefully back towards him till my back is flush against his chest. With his other hand he thrusts the rod in my face, shoving me with his torso. "Take it."

I clench my teeth and grip the rod. wanting to break it.

"Now, do it again." With another small shove he makes

sure I understand. With an irritated scowl I reel the line back. "There, happy now?"

His grip tightens and loosens against me like he's trying to say something without sounding too harsh. He kicks my legs outward a little and forces my knees to bend slightly as he pushes them with his own. The movement forces my body to lean further into his. I still as he releases me and his hands creep onto the rod and then onto mine. He places them then covers them with his before his entire body moves, taking mine with him, we roll backwards a fraction, my hands dance in the air in a delicate forceful arc. The wood bends and twists as we swing forwards, the line is unleashed, hissing as it travels over the water until it drops with a plop into the pond.

My heart ricochets in my chest as he keeps holding me, guiding my hands to the reel where slowly, I begin to draw back the line. Painstakingly slow. His hands guide mine, determining the pace until the empty line dangles free from the water.

He resets the rod, feeding a fresh maggot onto the hook, then grabs me again, helping me to lurch the line into the water. His body unglues itself from mine. I swallow slowly and stare into the translucent waters. I begin to draw back the line, slowly, just like he'd shown me. For some reason I want him to be proud of me, I want to show him that I've learned, that I can be taught.

The line tightens and suddenly it resists my gentle pull, unreeling at a mad speed. Dorian launches himself at me and places my hands on the reel where slowly we begin the task of reeling my catch in. I'm giddy with excitement. Sweat drips down my back and cements Dorian's hard chest to my back. I feel it rise and fall against me, his breathing uneven like mine. The line tightens and tugs till at last, it comes free of the water.

The fish hangs and flaps its useless body as it dangles helplessly on the line, his silver scales like a delicate plate of armour and still he is defenceless without the water. Dorian helps me to bring him in. The fish stares at his death, his big eyes bulging, scales glinting in the sun.

"I caught a fish." I grin at him. Something like childish pride swells in my chest and a feral sound between a shriek and a squeal manages to find its way out of my mouth. I'm giddy and excited and suddenly I'm in Dorian's arms, wrapped around his strong broad body. I search the veil that shields his face from mine, wanting so desperately to find his eyes, find approval, find *something*.

His arms come around me, drawing me to him. One hand sinks into my hair, and his face is inches from mine. I sense his eyes burning my face, searching just as much as I am. If it weren't for that stupid veil this would almost feel natural, exciting, but a moment later he remembers himself and lets out an annoyed growl before pushing away from me. I step back.

"Don't touch me." He sounds suddenly angry before grabbing the rod from me and untangling the fish from the hook. It flutters like a broken butterfly in his hands.

"Fine!" I hiss, baffled and a little hurt. What the fuck? "But I want you to put the fish back in the water. At least one thing should be able to get away from you." I glare at him.

His head tilts towards me, before he grabs the flapping fish by his tail and discards him. It hits the water with a splash and vanishes.

I leave without another word.

||||

DORIAN

Fuck! What the hell was that? I find myself wishing I could rip this veil off my face and expose myself to her, taste her. Allow myself to lose control, tear the clothes off her body and bury myself deep into her. My cock jerks in my pants at the memory of her soft body in my arms. She looks delicate like she could break, but I know she's strong and I'm the one who would break against her. I swallow hard, grinding my teeth. I bet she tastes like a sweet cherry pie, warm and syrupy with just the right amount of tang, and her moans would be the melting ice cream. Decadent and smooth.

I groan and feel my scalp itch again. Why do I want to touch this girl? Want to know what she feels like wrapped around my dick? I want to nibble her skin and look into her eyes as she explodes around me.

I drop the fishing rod and grab my half-hardened cock instead. Maybe this time I can make it work.

||||

JINX

Dinner is a quiet affair. Dorian keeps his thoughts to himself, and I just feel angry as I shred the grilled fish on my plate. I hate that it tastes so good and that it reminds me of our afternoon and that he pushed me away even though I felt his body react to mine, even though it felt right.

I slam my fork into the table as if it is an extension of my thoughts, angry and frustrated. "Dorian."

The cutlery on the other side of the curtain that divides us falls silent. "Yes?" His voice is as calm as the water on the pond was today and my skin prickles with agitation.

"Is there a way to cut our deal short?"

"Why do you ask?" I hear a slight spike in his voice.

"I've already told you, I want to go home."

At my words a chair scrapes against the floor and a heavy silence falls again.

"Dorian."

"I'm here."

"Answer me."

"Why do you want to leave? What do you have back there that you do not have here?"

"That's none of your business, just answer me."

"You first."

I grunt and rub my face, trying to erase some of my irritation so that I can think straight. I inhale and stare at the stupid fabric hanging from the ceiling, wondering if he can see me. "I have my freedom."

"You're free here."

I scoff. "We both know that's a lie."

"It's not," he says simply, and I feel like punching something.

"My freedoms here are limited to the boundaries of this house and your schedules." I elaborate to appease his pedantic ways.

"Let me ask you this then. If you were back home right now, what would you be doing?"

I know what he's trying to do. I clench my jaw and let my head fall back into the seat. I stare at the ceiling for a moment before I answer. "I'd be working on my schoolwork."

"And tomorrow night?"

"The same."

"And the night after that?"

"What's your point?"

"My point is that here – once your chores are complete – you get to spend a day in the garden or the library or watch sunsets or go fishing."

My breath freezes inside me and my eyes jerk over to the curtain between us.

He continues even as my lungs fight for air and I flounder like the fish in the pool "Here, you will never have to work another day."

"I don't want to stay here."

"Why?"

"Because no matter how you paint it, it's still a prison."

He sighs, exasperated. "Here you are freer than you've ever been or ever will be again."

"If you truly believe that, you're delusional as well as infuriating."

"Infuriating?" The way he asks it pulls my face into a frown and I shake my head. He can't be that obtuse.

"Yes. You're infuriating." I promise myself time to analyse the fact that he didn't question it when I called him delusional.

"I am many things but I don't think I'm infuriating."

I scoff. "Our deal, can we shorten it?"

"How do I infuriate you?" He once again ignores my question.

"No! I answered your question, now you answer mine – can we?"

"I don't see a way to make that work."

"Why?"

"There is nothing more you could give me in exchange."

The way he speaks makes me think of an adult speaking to a young child, choosing their words very carefully.

"Fine." I begrudgingly accept his answer.

After a few more seconds the clinking of cutlery resumes and I stare at my fish wondering if it was the same one I watched Dorian throw into the water.

Maybe it couldn't get away after all.

||||

DORIAN

Victor clears the plates and the taste of fish and lemon lingers on my tongue. "Jinx?"

"What?" she snaps.

"Would you like to watch another sunset with me?"

She's quiet for a while. I can hear her breathing, calming herself, preparing herself mentally, and I find myself stupidly bracing for her answer.

"Sure," she says eventually, but her tone tells me she is completely disinterested. I wonder where else she'd rather be. The thought makes my scalp itch and I run a long bony finger over the crumbling bald patch.

"Are you?"

"Am I what?"

"Sure?"

She exhales sharply. "A drink on a deserted fairy tale fucking balcony isn't a date."

I could, of course, throw her words back in her face, but for once I bite my tongue. "What would you like to do?"

"On our date?"

A shiver slides up my spine. *Our.* "Yes."

"I want to dance." Her voice issues a challenge, and I can't help but smile. She's testing me.

"One hour."

"Huh?"

"I'll see you for your dance in one hour."

19

DORIAN

"The truth does not change according to our ability to
stomach it." — Flannery O'Connor

I get Victor to push the furniture around in the lounge to
allow for a makeshift dance floor and dust the old vinyl
player. I picked it up in an antique shop, one that
housed a rumoured spell book – it ended up being nothing
more than a children's fairy tale book, but over the years some
rumours have held truths and I've chased them all down.

The owner was using it at the time, belting out some
Hendrix. He was old and his gnarled fingers made everything feel dirty when he touched it. He eyed me the entire
time I scanned the shelves looking for the book with his icy
blue eyes that I feared saw through my veil. Even then, at
the beginning, I already had to hide myself. If the tabloids
got wind of my transformation, my entire empire could've
collapsed. You can't have a business built on beauty when
you're not beautiful. In the end I sold the business for twice

its value and invested in blue chip stocks, I've never been a poor man.

He resisted at first when I asked to buy the turntable. But everyone has a price. I don't know why I bought it. Maybe I wanted to hurt him, – take away something that gave him joy – in the same way that it had been taken away from me. Why should I be the only one suffering?

I bought all his vinyls too and broke most of them on the way out, leaving a trail of black shards in my wake.

I stare at the thing, unused and rusty. It looks decrepit like the man who used to own it. Like me. I push the thought away.

I dig through the pile of vinyls and set a few aside wondering which Jinx would choose. The fact that I care fascinates me. But I do care. I'm interested in her thoughts and choices. In her. I tilt my head as I catch a reflection of my veil on the glass shelf, feeling at odds with myself.

Feeling.

Again.

I give Victor a few other instructions and tell him to keep to his room tonight, knowing it will eat him apart to think of me with her. I've seen the way he looks at her; probably much the same way I do.

I smile to myself as he leaves, then sit on my chair and wait. It's another odd sensation. Waiting – for a girl no less. I think of the poor idiots I've witnessed waiting and staring at clocks over the years, while I just had to nod to a girl by my side. Still for some reason I'm prepared to wait. It's not like she's late, but somehow it feels like a waste of time, waiting for another person when my own company has often been more than adequate.

I stare at the fire. The hot day has melted into another cool night, bringing with it a storm. I can feel it. There's a thin tension in the air that stretches out like an old elastic band over us, so tight till it will snap and bring a deluge.

She clears her throat and my head snaps to the archway where she stands. She's brushed her hair and set it loose, long black strands like ink cascade over her shoulders. She's wearing one of the new dresses I bought her, short, black and tight, plunging down the front. It hugs her shapely figure perfectly.

I can't help but track her body – when did it become so attractive? She bounces on her bare feet. My silence has made her uncomfortable.

"Would you like a drink?" I offer.

"Will you be having one also?"

I shake my head and she purses her lips slightly. "But you should anyway," I urge her.

"Okay." She accepts but sounds reluctant.

"What would you like?"

"A vodka lime please."

I raise an eyebrow then stand and go to the drink cabinet. Like much in this house, it has not been used in years and yet Victor has done a fine job stocking the small bath with ice. It jingles in the glass as I throw in a few cubes then pour her vodka.

She accepts the drink with a tight smile and takes a large sip.

"I make you nervous." It's a statement not a question and it startles her. She tries to cover up but her eyes are the size of saucers and her eyebrows have shot up.

"No." She shakes her head then inhales. "Yes."

"Still?"

She sets her drink down and stares at me, her eyes always trying to find their way beyond my veil. She tips her head and her eyes dip to the ground.

"How can I change that?"

"Let me see you." She doesn't hesitate as her gaze lands on me once more.

"Can we have that dance first?" I can see her hesitation, the tightness around her eyes and tightly pulled smile. "Or you can dance for me instead, if you like?"

She nods but doesn't answer, instead she goes to stand by the vinyls and runs her fingers over the covers. She picks one and lets it slide out of the cover then sets it onto the turntable. The room fills with a crackle of static before *Black Magic Woman* blares out.

She doesn't turn to face me, instead her body starts to move. Her round ass sways in slight movements and the rest of her body follows. She pushes away from the table and spins, facing me. She transforms in front of me, from an ordinary girl to someone sultry and sexy, who uses her hips to seduce, and her arms to invite. She's poetry in motion, enchanting and beautiful and try as I might, I can't peel my gaze away from her. Her body is designed to enchant, to move, to beguile.

The song ends and for a moment the only sound in the room is my beating heart that thrashes with her shallow breaths. The static of the vinyl cuts through the room and the song starts again.

"Join me?" She steps closer and reaches out to me.

I take her offered hand, my body already overwhelmed by her. She allows me to envelop her in my arms, and her body moves against me. Her head rests on my chest, and I suck in a sharp breath. Still, her arms come around me and we sway to the slow music which knits around us, pulling us closer.

The song ends again, and I know I should push her away, except I don't. Her body keeps leading mine and I let her as the song starts for a third time. She pulls her head away from my chest and her eyes search the veil where my face should be.

"Tell me about your parents," She says as our bodies swing to the melody.

"Why?"

"Why not? It's what people do."

"Talk about their parents?"

"Get to know each other." Her head shakes in a small movement of disbelief.

I sigh. Right. Is that the kind of thing 'normal' people really want to know about each other? "They were nice people."

"Nice?" She arches an eyebrow, and I tighten my arm around her waist.

I shrug. "They were away a lot, rich people often are."

"They're rich?"

"Obviously."

"How is that obvious?"

I think about her question. Hidden as I am, without a trace of my previous life, I guess it wouldn't be obvious. "To those who know who I am."

"And who is that?" she asks and runs a hand a little higher up my back The movement forces our bodies closer together.

"Not who I used to be."

She huffs and her face creases for a second. "Who did you used to be?"

"A liar."

"And who are you now?"

"I don't know."

She nods, taking in this new information. "What did you lie about?"

"It doesn't matter."

"Maybe it does to me."

"Why? Are you always honest?"

"I try to be."

"So you never lie?"

"Well—"

"You've never told anyone they looked good even when they didn't? Or that the food they made is delicious even when it tasted like shit? You've never faked an orgasm?"

"Of course I have – but it was necessary."

"So some lies are necessary?"

"That's not what I said." She defends her words.

"But it's what you mean." I keep poking at her.

"No." She releases me and bites her lower lip.

"No?"

"The truth sometimes hurts."

"So do lies and omissions."

"Yes, but sometimes keeping how we feel to ourselves saves a lot of heartache."

"Like the way you feel about being around me?"

She turns away and takes a step back, sucks in a breath, giving herself time to organise her thoughts.

"We are all a mixture of lies and truths. Sometimes lies come from a kind place. But omission seems somehow worse."

"How?"

"Because it is deception. A liar knows when he is lying. He can conceive and think of the details, and knows how to avoid being caught. But people who only speak half-truths to hide things or to deceive, well, there is an art to that, one that is thought out and is meticulous and therefore much more dangerous."

I take in her reasoning. She's not wrong. It takes a certain kind of skill to omit and twist the truth just enough so that the listener doesn't realise they have been fed a lie. "You think I am a master of such crafts?"

"You hide a lot."

"For your own good."

She scoffs. "A decision made by you on my behalf."

"For mine also." I let down a little of my guard and her eyes jerk back to my face, full of empathy. She wants so badly to understand.

"You've had your dance," she says. "Now let me see you."

"I've just shown you more of myself than I have many others."

She seems to be mulling the words over. "I want more."

I scoff. They always want more. Maybe she's not so different from everyone else after all.

"Please," she adds. and the way she asks makes something stir inside me. "You promised."

"Did I?"

"You said you wanted me to be more comfortable around you."

I slam my eyes shut and when I open them again I give her a slight nod. "Come."

I go to my chair and sit down. "Give me your hand."

She reaches out a shaky hand and I take it in my gloved one, wishing I could feel her skin, glowing with a few sunny days, no longer milky and white. Thunder crashes in the distance mimicking my heart that gallops in my chest as I slide her hand under the veil.

I swallow hard as the pads of her fingers touch my chin. A feather of a touch that sends my body reeling and my heart jack-knifing in my chest. She traces my jaw, a long slow line that maps out each imperfect bump and crevice, each new scar and ridge on my face. My fists clench by my sides, my nails bite into my skin even through my gloves.

She doesn't flinch. Not even as she moves up over my cheek. My jaw clenches. She's feeling too much, taking too much, and yet I don't dare stop her. I'm frozen by her touch.

Her fingers drift across the skin I know to be scarred and deformed. She finds the top of my lips, her soft fingers graze my flesh and in a moment of madness I open my mouth, sucking her fingers into it. Without thinking I run my tongue over her digits before she snatches her hand away. She stumbles backwards, her wide eyes glaring at where she knows my face to be, then turns and bolts from the room without another word.

I fall back into my seat, relishing the salty taste of her fingers, the lingering taste of soap and the feel of her skin on my tongue. I briefly let my mind wander to the feel of my fingers inside her, her warm slick heat and her soft delicate moans. My greedy cock is suddenly alive in my pants. I want to be angry at myself for fucking up this moment we had, but if I'm honest with myself, I'm not sorry at all. This briefest of tastes made me want even more, all of her. And whether she likes it or not, I'm going to take it.

||||

DORIAN

The bed swallows her up and she pulls the sheet over her slight body. The night is unusually humid and the thick duvet is set aside in a pile. She'll be asleep soon and I'll have to go downstairs and deal with the monsters. So this time I steal from her is precious to me. I need it.

I wait for her usual routine – for her to reach for the book and thumb through pages while her eyes light up and her hands worry her lips as she stifles her yawns. Till her eyes grow too heavy and she puts the book down and sleeps in seconds.

But tonight she ignores her book. Instead her eyes close and her hands crawl under the sheet. A faint draw of her breath as her back arches a few inches off the mattress. My breath hitches in my throat, and I glue myself to the wall, wanting to be inside the room. As one of her hands creeps lower down, pulling the sheet away with it, it slips inside the lacy underwear she wears, obscuring my view. It moves under the fabric, the muscles of her arm twitch and tense and she lets out a soft moan. Her back arches again and she rips at the shirt, exposing her breasts. Her fingers find the stiff rosy nipples and roll and tug. Shallow ragged breaths dry my lips. I want to lick them, but my mouth feels dry. I grip my hard cock and move along with her. Stroking the length of my shaft.

I wonder if she thinks of me as she touches herself. I want to be her hands, possess them as she speeds up. Watching her is bewitching, I'm under a spell. A strangled groan tumbles from her and everything inside me tightens. Her hips rock against her fingers and low moans tumble from her now, even as she bites down on her lower lip trying to seal them inside. The room is charged with her sex and sweat. I can taste it even here in my alcove. It seeps through the walls of the house and wraps itself around me. I tighten my grip, my strokes quickening. Her entire body is alive, her cheeks flushed, her eyes clenched shut, her hips rolling and her hands moving in a wild frenzy.

I have never watched a woman touch herself, never cared enough to see what their pleasure might look like, always chasing my own. Her abandon lights a fire inside me. I bite down on my lower lips to keep my grunts from escaping as my strokes speed up, mimicking her movements, fucking her in my head.

She is a great artist creating a masterpiece, layering paint in wild strokes, tiny details and vivid colour. She is an erotic Van Gogh. Her body shivers, every inch of her like she's experiencing an imminent implosion. And then she shatters. All her muscles tense and tremble, her back arches and a series of hungry desperate whimpers fall from her as her legs clench around her hand and her teeth dig into her lip. Her head whips back into the pillow, putting her long throat on display as she writhes on the bed.

My knees threaten to buckle as pleasure erupts inside my body and I come hard and fast, catching my cum in my shirt. I keep watching her, mesmerised, not wanting to miss a second, hating myself for being weak, for letting my eyes close, for needing to breathe more heavily. When the last of the shivers stop, she lays wasted and panting on the bed, a sheen of sweat on her forehead, her hair a tousled mess about her. I detest the underwear she wears, the fabric that obscures her from me.

She lets her hands fall by her side, and I lick my lips, wanting to taste her, willing her to taste herself. She lays motionless, her fuzzy dreamy gaze locked somewhere in her imagination. Breathing. Her beautiful bare breasts rise and fall with her breaths, and I crave to run my tongue all over them, to drag my teeth on her pale skin.

She sits up and lets the shirt cover her up then disappears into the bathroom. The knocking of pipes tells me she is washing herself. Disappointment flickers inside me a second before anger flares under my skin. I feel possessed by the need to have her like she's cast another wicked spell on me. This plain, imperfect girl is consuming my every waking hour, my need for her unquenchable.

I want her. And I will have her.

I keep watching till she falls into a deep sleep and,

without a thought or a care, I step into her room, hovering over her bed.

She's somehow grown more beautiful. Her raven black hair tousled about her, a slight blush to her cheeks, looking so peaceful as she breathes in and out in a rhythmic cadence.

Ever so slowly I raise my hand and feather my fingers from her temple to her cheek. She mumbles something, and I jerk my hand away. I wait, observing my sleeping beauty. My obsession. I'd never desired anyone before, never wanted so deeply, so desperately. She's somehow slithered under my skin and possesses me. And now I would possess her also.

My body throbs with eager desire for this creature who has set me on fire. My patience wanes. I know she's passed out for the night, and still, I'm hesitant. My hand wanders to her mouth and I pluck at her lip. It bounces at the touch and remains slightly open.

Temptation.

Invitation.

I grip her chin and bend closer. She smells like lilies. Her hot breath kisses mine as my tongue darts out and licks her lips. So plump. So sweet. A satisfied shiver crawls down my body, and I release her chin so that I can trace the length of her long neck, remembering how it corded when her head whipped back. I feel her swallow under my touch and excitement ripples inside me. She may be sleeping, but she knows I'm here. I drag my teeth along the flesh. She moans a little. And my cock swells.

Inching slightly away, I rip the blanket from her body. Goosebumps erupt on her exposed skin and I wonder what it is about her that makes me crave her so much. That makes me want to make her mine. It was only a game, a fool's errand, and now she's all I want. Perhaps it is because she resists me; I've never had to work hard for anything let alone attention, affection. Her resistance makes me want to break her in like a wild animal. I know how wild she is. How she could be.

I push her shirt up and study her naked torso. She is intoxicating, breathtaking. My fingers reach out as if not a part of my body. They feather her naked skin, stroking, circling, tugging. She shifts and moans, and I relish in the feel of her. So soft. So fucking delicate, like a china doll. Except I know I can't break her.

I fall to my knees at the side of the bed and allow myself one taste of her nipple. Sucking it into my mouth like a strawberry on a winter's day. I drag my teeth along the hard rosy flesh and we groan in unison. My body shudders, the urge to relieve her of her clothes and take her without her knowledge is a temptation almost too hard to resist. But not like this. Tonight, I just want a taste. When she comes to me, I want her to do it willingly. I need her to choose me.

My fingers circle her belly button and glide to the lining of the lacy underwear. Loose against her thin frame. They slide beneath the elastic and find the coarse hair that adorns the apex of her thighs. They dip further still till I feel her heat and wetness. Even in her sleep, she wants me.

I groan at the feel of her warmth. I can't help but caress her, allow my fingers to travel up and down, to tease her, and she moans again, her breathing gradually changing, becoming shallower, her hips rise to meet me.

I can't help but grin, satisfaction washing over me. Her face twitches, her body knows I'm here, wants me. I pull my finger back. And watch as her breathing is once again heavy and rhythmic.

I bring my fingers to my nose and smell her scent, memorising it, delighting in it before putting my fingers in my mouth. I taste her again. Revelling at her salty and sweet deliciousness, just as I remembered.

I wonder how much sweeter she will taste when she finally surrenders herself to me, when she finally admits that she wants this. Me. When she willingly bucks beneath me and meets my needs.

I stand up, taking a final lingering glance at my tormentor, then spread the blanket over her and leave the room.

20

JINX

"The truth will set you free, but first it will piss you off."
— Joe Klaas

I want to hide but of course I can't, my chores force me out of my room. I complete my arduous tasks, but today I don't feel him anywhere. The sensation is odd and hollow. I don't even know why I care.

I find him hunched over the table, reading in his library. He barely looks up when I walk in and grab a book from the shelf. I need to pace myself, time my questions just right. We continue our reading, neither of us mentioning how our 'date' ended, instead choosing to bury ourselves in silence and research. I wonder what the beautiful monster thinks when I feel his gaze weighing down on me. I allow him a certain closeness that I didn't before. Somehow seeing him with my hands alone has given me reassurance about his intentions with me. A safety I didn't think he could offer.

After a long while, I set the book aside and rub my tired eyes. Who knew there was so much magic in the world?

"There's nothing relevant in this one, not unless you are infested in maggots and cancer?"

"No." He sounds amused.

"Well that's a relief."

"Is it?"

"Isn't it?"

"I guess."

"You guess? Would maggots and cancer be better than your curse?"

"Both have easy cures."

"Easy?"

"Well... at least the maggots do."

I twist my face in disgust and he chuckles at my expression. "What about this one?"

"Well?" He's at my side. I can sense his eagerness in the way his muscles tense and his neck cranes over my shoulder, seeking a glimpse.

"Right here." I point to the incantation written on the page, and he snatches the book from my hands.

He skims over it. "A wishing spell?" He turns back to me.

"Yes, just wish your curse away."

He scoffs and throws the book on the table dismissively. "That's ridiculous."

I frown, irritation skittering along my neck. "It's not. It makes perfect sense."

"If it was that easy, I would have done it by now."

"You can't be sure till you've tried."

He doesn't respond.

"Have you?"

"Have I what?" He plays stupid, but we both know what I am asking.

"Have you tried?"

"Yes, I have tried just about every fucking thing under the sun!" His voice thunders in the small room and bounces off the walls. His tone leaves no room for questions.

I grind my teeth and stare at this man who hides in plain sight. He's so close I can touch him, smell him, and if I asked, I could probably taste him in the same way he's tasted me. And yet I can't see him. Not like I thought I could. A new version of him suddenly appears in my head, and I shiver, the old fear creeping back inside me.

"How long?'

"How long what?"

"How long have you been cursed?"

"I don't know."

"Dorian—"

"It's the truth," he cuts me off, "years, decades, centuries? It's hard to tell, time moves differently for you than it does for me, I know the world has changes around me, but not much, but at the same time my body feels strong, but as if it has been alive for hundreds of years. This curse feels time-less, limitless." He sighs and for s single moment seems to shrink, "All I want is for it to end."

"If you know how to break your curse, then what the hell are we doing here? What haven't you tried? Every spell and charm, every suggestion I have, you throw back in my face."

"Jinx—"

"No, I'm tired of your shit. If you have the answer, just tell me what it is. I'm sick of wasting my time here."

"With me?" He sounds dejected, but part of me wants to hurt him. Wants him to feel an iota of the pain he's given me.

"That's not how I meant it," I grind out, uncertain about my honesty. "I just meant that it feels like we're going around in circles and that you know more than you let on."

He remains silent, as he often does when telling me the

truth would implicate him somehow. He thrives on omissions.

I bite my lower lip, holding my frustration inside. "Fine, about our deal—"

His sigh cuts me off. "Will be over soon..."

"I know." I can't curb the enthusiasm in my voice.

"I don't want you to leave."

"Why?"

He crosses the room in three swift steps that make it seem as if he'd floated across the room. "We haven't finished our research."

"The 'research'? Is any of it even real?" I don't try to hide the bitterness in my voice.

He doesn't answer me.

Shocker.

"That's all?"

The silence stretches between us. Getting thicker and darker like the threatening sky. "I've grown fond of your company," he finally says.

"Fond?"

"I like spending time with you, you're... interesting."

"Interesting?"

"Yes."

"Well... thanks, I guess. This whole place is interesting." I wave my hands around me.

He barks out a sad laugh. "Not how I would describe it."

"How would you describe it then?"

"I won't." He ends my line of questioning with his abrupt answer. I turn to leave, but his voice grabs me back. "You could stay, I could pay you. You could continue to help me with my research."

"I already have a job."

"This one would pay better."

"I don't think that's a good id—"

"It would be easier too."

I find his face, hoping that somewhere between us our eyes meet. "I'm not sure it would be."

"So you'd rather be cleaning toilets than spending time with me?" All his softness vaporises and his tone is icy and cold. "You want to leave so badly? My presence bothers you so much? Leave then!" he roars at me, and I flinch a little. But we both know I won't, can't, not without my work.

"My work..." I start, but he cuts me off with a snarl.

"This? This is what you want?" He holds a stack of papers in his hand, and I lunge out to reach for it. "This is all you care about?" He easily swings out of my reach and storms out of the room, his left leg dragging slightly with an uneven limp I haven't noticed before.

Of course, what else would I care about? If he thinks I am here for any other reason he is more deranged than I gave him credit for. Isn't he? I mean why else would I possibly want to stay?

I go after him. "Give me my work."

He's in the lounge room and rushes towards the fire-place. Suddenly my heart is in my throat and his intentions are clear. "You want to go so badly? Go!" he screams at me as he releases the papers in his hands and they fall like feathers into the burning hearth.

"No!" I screech, it's feral and loud and savage. My heart slams in my chest and I scramble to save my work as the fire begins to lick the pages, each one recoiling from the heat, wrinkling and folding in on themselves as one by one they succumb to the flames. "Move!" I scream at him as he blocks each of my attempts at reaching the fire, saving my work, my words.

With a final puff, the pages crumble, filling the hearth with tiny golden embers.

"What did you do?" I am consumed with white rage, the

likes of which I have never felt before. Every part of my body feels alive with hatred. I want to see his eyes, to burn through them with my own, but he looks at me silently through that fucking veil, his mask, his precious hideaway.

But I know what else is precious to him. I know what I can take away.

I swivel and run back to the library where he keeps his priceless maps and books and 'research'.

"I'm warning you, Jinx, don't do anything you might regret." His voice slithers behind me, but I am too far gone to be afraid of his threats.

Thunder rumbles above us as a maniacal laugh rips from me and I take another step towards the desk. "Something *I* might regret? Like coming to live in this house? Like trusting you? Like thinking you are something different than what you clearly are?" I gasp for breath. "I know plenty about regret." I bristle and he says nothing.

I'm out of patience. I bound to his desk and throw myself at the maps and books, at the neatly stacked piles of papers and ornaments. Books thump on the floor like thunder and paper flies like parchment rain as my body sticks to maps, the ink running and imprinting itself onto my shirt.

"Stop." I hear his voice but I don't stop. My hands have a mind of their own as they scatter and push and destroy.

The pain is harsh and sharp and lances through my shoulder as I'm whipped off the table and thrown into the wall. The air leaves my lungs in a brutal exhale and my cheek bounces off the wooden panel.

"You shouldn't have done that," Dorian's voice snaps in my ear as his body pins mine against the wall. His hard chest pushes against my back, forcing my cheek to kiss the cold wooden panels.

I pant, catching my breath, my heart ricocheting in my

chest. "Let go of me!" I push against the wall, but Dorian's bigger, stronger body holds me down.

"No."

"Let go. I'm tired of being your prisoner."

He laughs, his body shakes against me. "The only prison you're in is inside your head."

I try and push against him again. "Get the fuck off me."

"Why?"

"I. Hate. You." I grind it out slowly and meticulously, each word an arrow laced with venom.

"I don't think you do." The venom in his voice slithers inside me. "You hate that you can't control everything, you hate that you don't get what you want when you want it, you hate that even though you won't admit it, you like being here, with me. You like it when I touch you, you crave it."

"You're wrong."

"Really? Is that why you spend all your time here with me? Bend over like a good slut when I tell you to?"

I shudder against him. "Maybe I like a good freak show."

"Careful, Jinx."

"Or else what? What are you going to do? Keep hiding? You're the one who's the control freak. Hiding in stupid shadows, talking in circles, trying to break down my walls and get into my heart without showing yours. It doesn't work like that, asshole."

"What makes you assume I want your heart?" His hands glides across my waist and band around my hip, pulling me to him. I can feel his hard cock as it grinds against my ass. "Maybe all I want is to get into your pants."

"You wouldn't dare! Our deal's off." But even as I say it, heat pools between my legs and I instinctively arch myself into him. Hatred boiling over into desire.

"Tell me to stop then." His hand creeps under my singlet

and a gloved finger scratches the skin just below my belly button.

I suck in a breath and feel his burning my neck. I stay silent as his hand slides into my underwear and his fingers slide into my wetness.

I gasp at the intrusion, at the touch, at the pleasure.

"I don't think you hate me at all, Jinx." He yanks at the elastic of my underwear and pushes them down. They cling to my legs and come to rest midway up my thighs.

"Fuck you, Dorian."

"I think you'd like me to do just that." He pushes into me, letting me feel the hard length of his cock before he releases me.

I take the opportunity to spin around and hit his chest with my fists. He laughs, then easily grabs my hands and pins them above me, forcing my body up, pulling at my shoulders till I have to stand on my tiptoes to ease the pain. "You're not putting up much of a fight are you, Jinx? Tell me, do you still want to pretend that you hate me?"

"I do," I bark back. His free hand latches on to a nipple and he tugs. I fucking moan. And worse, I arch into his hold.

"So why aren't you stopping me?" he asks as he pulls down his pants, releasing his hard cock. I can't help but look, catching myself licking my lips. Whatever his curse, it clearly did not affect his cock. I try to back up into the wall and I catch his scoff from behind his veil.

I make an attempt to kick up but lose my footing, my shoulders stretch and ache. "Get off me!" I cry out as he spins me around again and slams me into the wall. His hands slip between my thighs, ripping a moan from my mouth.

"Are you sure? Cause it feels to me like you want this just as much as I do."

I want to push him away but instead, I grind against the

pressure of his fingers on my clit. My anger dissolves into need, need into a hungry craving. And I push myself against him.

I hate him.

I want him.

Before I have another chance to protest or fight, he lines his cock up and slams into me. I cry out, the line between pleasure and pain, a thin delicious blur. He stills inside me for a beat, his fingers digging into my flesh. His chest expands with his sharp intake of breath and a low growl escapes, making my heart kick up.

It's the thunder that wakes his beast, and he pulls back and slams back inside me, thrusting back and forth, setting a brutal pace. I can't help but push back to meet his thrusts. I hate him. I don't want his hands to feel this good and for my body to react to him the way it does. But still, I moan for him, meeting him thrust for thrust, wanting all of him, deeper harder, needing to let the hate consume me. It makes me burn. His hand slips down to my pussy, and I chase the pleasure it offers, my pulse hammering as pleasure builds inside me.

I allow the monster to chase away my demons. I'm a sinner, and the way his body makes mine feel makes me want to scream my confession. So I do, I moan for him as my orgasm builds, an angry desperate tempest that shatters through my body, till the pleasure that lurks inside consumes me. His hips stutter and he thrusts into me twice more before stilling, releasing my arms at last and wrapping himself around my hips forcing himself deeper as I crave more of him.

I pant against the wall, my breath fogging up the wooden panel, my sweat-drenched shirt growing cold as Dorian rips himself from me. I spin, my back to the wall.

Wanting his face, wanting his eyes, instead, all I get is a fabric shroud that hides him.

I snarl at the cloaked man and slap his face. I know it connects. "Coward!" I snap at him.

I rush out of the library and upstairs, slamming the door to my room. Pressing against it, my heart chugs and emotion clogs my throat.

Fuck.

||||

Water drips in rivulets down my face as I splash it for a third and fourth time, washing away the feelings that war inside me. How the hell did I allow that to happen? Allow this man who holds me captive to touch me like that, to make my body feel like that? When did all my hatred turn into something else? Or had it at all? I shake my head, wanting to rid myself of these thoughts, of the feel of him inside me, of his harsh strokes and blunt words.

Did a part of me want to stay? It doesn't matter. I am stuck here. Right? I don't really have a choice. Except that now, I do – he burned my fucking pages. I saw them go up in flames. Anger seeps back under my skin and burns my face.

I storm back into my bedroom and open the top drawer of the bedside table. My car keys are gone. I close the drawer and pull it open a second time as if they might reappear; they are not where I left them. I rummage through the drawers of my nightstand, emptying them mindlessly onto the floor. They are mostly empty apart from a few useless trinkets Dorian included in his bag of clothes. When I come up with nothing, my heart kicks up and my insides constrict.

I scour every inch of the room, my eyes darting feverishly from one corner to another.

I leave the mess on the floor and move to my backpack, unpacking it with little grace and shaking it frantically, releasing empty gum papers, an old capless pen, three coins and a collection of dust mites onto the floor.

Frustration tightens its grip around my throat and I suck in a lungful of air before I move to my closet.

My trembling hands dive into the depths of my closet, yanking clothes from hangers, rummaging through pockets. Still nothing. Kneeling on the floor, I sift through shoes and discarded clothing, but despite my desperate search I come up empty.

Their absence gnaws at my sanity, pushing me further into the depths of desperation. I know what he did, and maybe my next move is more an act of rebellion than necessity.

I flip the mattress, sending pillows and blankets flying.

The room, once an oasis of calm, now mirrors the chaos inside my mind. I toss aside the pillows, and upturn any piece of furniture I can lift, caring little for the consequences of my frenzy. Sweat drips down my forehead, my breath ragged as I fight back tears.

I don't know how much time passes when exhaustion finally settles in, and I scan the room one last time.

I don't have the energy to face him, to battle, to scream, and so I fall onto the discarded mattress, hopelessness overtaking me like lost asteroids in a vast empty space on a doomed trajectory, inevitably leading to a tragic end.

Tomorrow. I'll get out of here first thing tomorrow.

21

JINX

"The truth is a beautiful and terrible thing, and should therefore be treated with great caution." — J.K. Rowling

I wake with a start and scramble to the back of the bed, clutching the blanket to my chest. A thin film of sweat covers my body and that unshakable feeling of being watched follows me around. I search the room as my eyes adjust to the dim light, but no one is there. Instead, my eyes find a short stack of papers, five to be exact. I reach out and grab them, skimming the words, *my* words. My pages, my stories, those I thought he burned last night sit and wait for me as my payment.

I grind my teeth – that fucker tricked me, but also, he gave me what is mine, as he always has. The urge that gripped me the night before, the one that wants me to run out the door and never look back trickles slowly away from me. He still has my work – *all of it*. I still belong to him, and maybe if I am truthful and don't try to examine things too deeply, I don't entirely mind.

I climb out of the bed and walk to the window, staring at the dark angry sky. Lightning rips through the black curtain and sets the world alight. Angry thunder roars above, threatening, as it has for days now, building like the fury inside me. Everything around me feels as though it wants to snap, and break, come completely apart.

My thoughts patter around my head like scattered lost sheep and my arms wrap around me like rope, the cold air doing little to clear the fog inside my head. The murky confusion, the anger colliding with gratefulness, the gratitude with hatred, the hatred with lust.

Fuck, what did I get myself into?

||||

DORIAN

Today I will mend things. Now that I know she wants me, I know I'm a lot closer to the end game. To get everything I want. And I'm discovering that I want so many things when it comes to Jinx. Of course, I want my cock to work again just as it did yesterday, I want to conquer again – and I want this curse to come to an end. That is the ultimate prize, but there are so many other stops along the way that I find myself wanting to make.

I want to taste her again. Everything tastes bland without her flavour. I feel deprived, hungry – more than that – I am fucking starving. I want to sink myself into her and see her face when she comes, I want her to call out my name, I want to spend time worshipping her perky little tits till she begs me to stop. I want to master her, and make her unquestionably mine. And then I would have done one real thing in this lifetime.

My whole body hardens as I sit for breakfast with the thought, my appetite for food almost entirely gone as I know what I need to do, and wonder if my little guest will indulge me.

I wait for her in the library, my body tense and taut as I think about all the ways I could have her here. The thought makes my cock jerk and my lips twitch. When she walks in, she looks right at me. I like that she doesn't shy away from our deeds. I like that she owns it.

"Where the hell are my car keys?" She doesn't mince her words, I like that about her.

"Victor moved your car out of the elements and to the main garage. They are hanging in the kitchen with the rest of the keys, you can take them any time."

"Oh." She almost shrinks a little.

"Did you sleep well?" I divert.

"No, of course not."

"But why?" I know why, but I feel like getting under her skin.

"You know why."

"I don't."

"You tricked me."

"You saw what you wanted to see."

"You didn't have to do that."

"But look at where it got us."

The muscles of her jaw dance around as her eyes sweep the room. She says nothing else.

"Did you get a chance to eat breakfast?"

"I did, thanks." She keeps her distance, keeping the large table between us then grabs a book still lying open on the floor.

"Good, you will need your strength for your chores

today." Her head snaps up and her eyes grow big as she stares at me.

"Chores?"

"Yes, your chores."

She huffs as if expecting a different answer.

When she says nothing else, I continue, "You will earn your pages today by cleaning up the mess you made here last night."

"I—?"

"Yes."

She did do some damage. I can't repair the maps or retrace the ink, and even though everything in here has been digitised and preserved, I still feel like she should be punished for destroying such precious, rare resources.

And I intend to.

It's okay.

Eventually, she'll come around. Isolation is a brutal mistress that breaks even the most resilient.

I thought I was strong once. Before I cast myself to this place. The aloneness seemed necessary. At first, it healed. It allowed me to venture around freely in my own deformed state without the worry and stress of being spotted or seen. But the silence became too loud, an emptiness which hid in every cupboard and every corner. Till all that I had was the sound of my blood rushing around my body and the constant thud of my heartbeat echoing off the empty walls. It was then that Victor found me. We are both monsters. I know Victor and Jinx think they are captives, but I am the only one who will never truly be free.

I am lost in thought when somewhere in the house the clock chimes eleven, and when I rip my eyes from the book I haven't been reading, I find Jinx finishing up her task. The room is spotless; she has dutifully managed to erase any trace of yesterday's misdeeds.

"When you are done, we will read in the library."

Her mouth falls slowly open. "But I usually read after dinner."

I ignore the waver in her voice. "I'll be waiting." Scraping myself out of the chair, I brush by her, feeling her hot glare as I do. "You missed one," I say as I leave the room, pointing to the book I left on the chair.

She is seething when she comes to the lounge. The anger pours off her in heat waves, like the aftershocks of an explosion. They radiate across the room and lick my skin. I let them. Her anger only forces her to feel things, to desire things – like me. I feed her monster.

She halts as she rounds the chair, not expecting me to be sitting in it. A worried expression crosses her face for a second before she manages to conceal it. I let her watch me as I untuck my shirt and undo the button of my pants. When I'm done, I grab the three sheets of paper I brought with me and turn to look at her. She just keeps standing there, waiting for a nudge of some sort, but I wait, letting her connect the dots.

Slowly but surely her eyes grow bigger as they sweep over me, my covered face down to my open button and the way I am leaning slightly uncomfortably on the edge of my seat my knees sprawled wide.

"Go on."

"But..." She swallows hard. "I can't read with..." Her words drop away, and I hold back my chuckle.

"Don't worry about it, I'll be reading today," I reassure her and wait for her to come, knowing full well she will.

I watch her try to contain all her emotions behind a blank face, but she can't hide everything. The loathing, the panic, the slight but definitely-there curiosity. She stops directly in front of me, her eyes set firmly on the bulge in my pants.

Jinx drops onto one knee, then the next, each movement slow and deliberate. I wait, maybe a part of me still thinks she will say no, maybe a part of me hopes she will, but then her hand reaches over to my pants. She hovers for a few seconds, still unsure before reaching over and slowly undoing my zip. She could have of course pulled it right down but she's stalling and the anticipation is getting me harder, more excited. The slower she goes the harder I get and my cock pushes against the black boxers.

Her eyes flick up to me. I'm unsure if she's waiting for me to end this or waiting for permission. I end her doubts. "Take it out."

Her jaw twitches as if she wants to protest or say something, but she remains quiet while her face saturates with a lovely shade of red. It spreads from her ears to her cheeks and down her neck. Lovely.

She lifts the waistband of my boxers and pushes it down past my cock, letting the elastic fit below my balls. I don't miss the tiny gasp and the way her pupils dilate. I'm fucking beaming as it stands hard and swollen, just like it used to. Fuck this woman does things to me I'd forgotten were possible.

Jinx reaches over and wraps one of her hands around the shaft, and I can't help the hiss that slithers from my lips. It makes her hand tighten for a split-second, and I glare down at her as she gives my cock a few experimental strokes, like she's testing the weight and girth. Or maybe she is buying herself more time. I don't give a shit, I've already achieved more than I thought I could with her, and the fact that she is choosing to have her hand on my dick spurs me on to believe that she will choose to swallow it, over and over again. Giddy anticipation runs down my body as she strokes again.

"Read." Her raspy voice sucks me from my thoughts as

her hot breath skates over the head of my cock a second before she sucks it into her mouth. I groan, and for a split-second I see her eyes light up like suddenly she thinks she has some sort of control over the situation.

I start reading, but as I do Jinx tightens her fist around my shaft and feeds my entire cock into her mouth. I shudder at the delight. I try to read once more – a story about a frog and a spoiled princess. The words churn from my mouth mechanically as Jinx works my cock, using her hand to feed me deeper into her mouth and the other to play with my balls. She has me on edge as I continue forcing the words from my mouth – the princess would not keep her promise to the fucking frog and I don't give any shits at all but I don't want her to stop, so I don't either.

I pop out of her mouth and she uses her tongue to lick me from balls to tip, and though it feels incredible, I want to be back inside her mouth. I don't dare move though, give any indication at all that the sudden loss of her mouth has affected me.

Her mouth moves down to my balls and she sucks one into her mouth. I can't help the growl that rushes from me. She doesn't react, just sucks while her fist strokes my cock, keeping me on edge before she sucks me back down to the very back of her throat. She holds before doing it again and again, her efforts doubling, saliva sliding from her mouth and pooling down to my balls.

I take a breath, my eyes no longer focused on the words but on her. She notices and when she pulls away she looks right at me as if she can see through the veil and into my eyes. Hers are wide and her mouth is open and I watch every inch of myself slide out from between her lips till I pop out. She runs her tongue over her lips. "Read, Dorian."

I stare at this creature who thinks that she can tell me what to do in my home, that thinks she has any control here.

I suck in a long breath and lean in. "Put your hands behind your back."

"What?"

"You heard me, hands behind your back, Jinx."

She looks at me again – that fear and curiosity back across her features. I wait as she loops one hand around her back and then the other. She looks at me.

"You're not done," I growl, and wait.

Her jaw tightens again and she clenches her thighs together. Little Jinx might be enjoying this more than she lets on. She leans forward again, and despite the awkward angle, takes me into her mouth.

Grinding my jaw, I find my place on the page – the place where the frog becomes a prince that punishes the spoiled princess – the place where he curses her. Fucking fairy tales and curses. I grit my teeth and slam the pages down, sliding a hand into her hair and fisting the strands. Her eyes lift up at me, but I don't give her a chance this time. I dictate the pace, slow and steady, without interruptions. She gags, and each time she does my cock throbs a little more as her throat closes around it. The more she gags the longer I hold her down, watching her nostrils flare and her eyes water. I keep expecting her hands to come up and tear mine from her hair but they never do.

I keep pumping my cock into her mouth, harder now, pushing her boundaries and rediscovering mine till all I feel is that one point of focus – the pleasure that builds in my back and travels to my balls – and without thought I come hard into the back of her throat, pumping myself into her, forcing her mouth to close around me and accept every last drop while she chokes and gags.

I pull her head up, and she stares at me, her mouth sealed. "Swallow."

Her throat bobs as my cum slithers down her throat. I can't take my eyes off her.

I release her hair and she falls back, her hands coming to rest by her sides. She scrambles to her feet as if wanting to flee the scene of a crime. I grab her wrist. "Wait."

"I did everything you said." Her words rush through heavy breaths.

I ignore her as I pull her closer to me. My hands creep up to her thigh and she gasps as I slip under the elastic of her underwear. Even through my gloves I can feel how wet she is, how very fucking saturated she is. I run my fingers over her clit, and she sucks in a breath each time I do, her wrist tugging in my hold. I pull away and let her go.

"Are we done?" I nod and hold up her papers. She snatches them from my hand and storms out of the room.

22

DORIAN

"Tell the truth, or someone will tell it for you." —
Stephanie Klein

The day drags without Jinx. She's holed up in her room, avoiding me again, and somehow the house that has been able to shut out the world and keep my secrets safe, suddenly feels like a gaping empty hole I struggle to fill. All I want is to be near her. I want her noise to fill my silent existence. The realisation has me reeling, questioning everything I have always believed to be true about love and its existence, but more crucially, my ability to feel it towards another person.

Her.

Jinx.

She is so imperfect, nothing about her screams of beauty and perfection; parts of her are broken and desperate and yet – I want her, all of her, from the scarred skin and light wrinkles, the curves, and that mouth of hers, the one that talks back and gets under my skin, the one that swallowed my cock the afternoon before and drove me to the brink. My body quivers with the memory and heat stings my skin making it feel tight and needy.

I release the air in my lungs in a slow exhale and stare at the clock. Eventually she will get bored and come down here as she always does, and when she walks in I'll find it hard to keep my hands off her, because occupying the same space as her is becoming harder and harder and my self-control is slipping every day. My eyes slip over the copy of the story I read the night before. Jinx has no idea how her words affect me, her stories, the morals she tries to instil inside them, each word gutting my insides deeper than the next, as if she's taken a mirror into my life and is forcing me to look. I slam the desk with a fist. I hate mirrors and I hate her; she wants me to believe in something I can't have.

I can't say I blame her, not after yesterday, not after she swallowed my cock with such fervour, not after her teary eyes searched for mine, not after she swallowed every last drop. My fists clench tightly and my long nails bite into my dry grey skin.

Being around her makes parts of me surface, parts I didn't even know existed and some that have been dormant for so long I've forgotten how much pleasure I used to derive from them.

The commanding, demanding part of me, the part that knows it would be obeyed, the part that likes to make demands and have them met instantly. And Jinx, she obeys, despite the uncertainty in her eyes, despite the wariness and fear, she does what she is told, braving it anyway and as far as I can tell, *enjoying it*. That was dangerous, for both of us. I've always enjoyed flexing my power over others and she feeds those parts of me that want more. It makes me question how far I could push her, how far she would let me go before she comes to her senses and runs.

The day keeps ticking away. The house fills with the aroma of wood polish and disinfectant. She does her chores like a good little worker, but she doesn't come to the library. I can't say I blame her, and if I am truthful, I am also relieved.

I read over her story for the fourth time that day, the frog prince and how he called his curse a gift to the beautiful princess, plunging her into a life of ugly despair. Forcing her to see the world from a new perspective, a world where people like me look down at her before giving her a chance, a world where outer beauty determines a pathway for you whether we know it or not, a world where a marred face is a curse. I clutch the arm of the chair in one hand and crumple the story in the other, watching the papers become nothing more than a balled-up memory I discard them. Not that it matters, her words have already etched themselves into me.

When the clock strikes six, I suck in a lungful of stale air and make my way to the dining room.

||||

JINX

"How was your day?" His voice filters through the curtain between us, and I look up at the fabric and sigh. It's like talking to a wall, an invisible man. I hate it.

"It was fine." I don't have the patience for pleasantries today, nor the nerves. My stomach has been a tightly knit ball of anxiety since the day before, and the sheer thought of what's next is eating me alive. How much further will he push, what else will he demand, and more to the point, what will I allow myself to do? How much more of me am I willing to give? I swallow down the truth.

"I read over your story about the frog and the curse again today."

My head jerks up. "How?"

The silence stretches long and thick between us and I think about the story, about *his* curse, about the man he used to be. Was he much the same? Or is he now a product of his curse? I've spent so much time locked up in the library with Dorian. When he's not being a condescending dick he's actually extremely intelligent and I find glimpses of humour and charm. This story feels so poignant but brings about so many questions I know he won't answer, but I try anyway. "Is that how you feel?" I find my voice but even to me it sounds frail and broken. "Like a frog in a world full of princes?"

He remains silent and I try again. "Do you think of your curse as a gift?"

"It wouldn't be called a curse if it was a gift now, would it?" He has that tone again, the one that suggests I haven't spent enough time getting an education. I ignore it and trudge on.

"You know what I mean. Was someone trying to teach you a lesson?"

"Why do you write these?" As always he answers with his own question, one that has nothing to do with my own.

I sigh, exasperated. "It's for school."

"Are they really?" I hate how perceptive he is and that he won't let this go till I give him the answer he wants. The truth.

"My father used to tell me stories before bedtime."

"What sort of stories?"

"Fairy tales."

"These are not fairy tales."

"They are, in their truest form. The villain is never who you think it is and the lesson is always harsh and cold."

"Real life is harsh and cold, why would a father tell these stories to a kid?"

"He didn't tell me *these* stories, his fairy tales had happier endings." At that, there is a shuffle and movement behind the curtain, and once again I can feel his focus set on my face even without seeing his eyes.

"So why don't yours?"

"Because his stories were full of lies. Life isn't full of happily-ever-afters, the good guys rarely win and tend to finish last."

"Wow. Who pissed in your breakfast?"

"The same person who pissed in yours when she cursed you," I bite out. It's unintentional, but he provoked me. He shouldn't be asking these questions, he shouldn't be dredging up the past or the stories of my father, all it will do is unearth the pain, the empty void they left behind.

He sits frozen, anger rolling off his solid form. It's a cold anger that threatens to freeze everything in the room.

"My father was a liar." I chip at the icy silence between us. Dorian doesn't move. My confession seems to pique his interest.

"What did he lie about?"

"Everything."

"That tells me nothing."

"And neither do you!" I snap at him, the last of my patience withering away.

I sit seething in silence, my dinner no longer appealing.

"Answer my questions and I'll answer yours." My head jerks up once more. I want to believe him, I want my answers. I nod, knowing he can see me, and search for a way

I can tell him, a way I can gouge at my own scars and make them bleed for him.

"What did he lie about?"

I swallow as the question hangs over me like a noose. My eyes fall down to my fingers that fidget and push each other around. "He lied about my mother, why she left."

He says nothing else, just allows me to talk. "His stories were always about a princess rescued by a prince, he likened them to my mum and him, saying he'd rescued her from her home, from poverty, from despair, that he treated her like a queen, gave her everything she ever wanted. In his stories the princess and the prince live together forever in a big castle, they had a baby girl that they loved more than either of them could ever say, and all his stories ended up with a version of me in their arms as they dote over me.

"But the truth of it was that there was no rescue. She was taken from her home as debt and forced into my father's bed. He was not a kind man, he was not a good man, and he stole her life and her joy and forced himself on her, till she gave him me. My memories of her are so faint most days, but sometimes I think I can hear her voice in my dreams."

My lip quivers as I push out my story. "When she vanished my dad told me she had gone on a holiday and that she would be back, that he had sent her away to rejuvenate. We both noticed how sad she was, emaciated and tired. It was the depression and desperation that ate her alive, and over time he'd limited our time together, trying to sever our bond. For years I believed him till I found her letter. Till I found the truth in her shaky handwriting."

I gulp down the sadness that closes my throat and push out the last of my story. "She ran away. My father was not a good man, he poisoned people with his drugs, he built an empire on lies and deceit, he promised people dreams and delivered nightmares. But he didn't just deal in drugs, he dealt in lives. People vanished in the night and woke up belonging to others. He groomed, broke and polished them before delivering them like they were goods. I don't know why he wanted my mother for himself, she didn't either, but she found a way to escape and promised to come for me too. She knew what he had planned for me despite all his promises. My mother never came back, and I ran out of time."

My words hang above us like frozen, sharp icicles. His snaps them away. "So you're hiding."

"I'm not cowering away in a broken house, if that's what you're asking."

"No, and I do not cower." I hear the undercurrent of anger in his voice and know I've hurt him. "Is your name even Jinx?"

This time I ignore him. I've answered his questions, now he needs to answer mine. "Tell me, does your curse feel like a gift? Do you feel like a frog in a world full of princes?"

His chuckle is low and sad, and I feel a momentary stab of guilt, but it evaporates as quickly as it's felt.

"Perhaps the only gift has been to remove me from the world and away from everyone else."

His answer is unexpected. "Your curse is to be alone?"

"No, I choose that for myself."

"Because of who you are?"

"Because of what I have become. But that was just the beginning, the edge of the sword. What really eats you alive is the loneliness."

"Why don't you return to the world?"

He scoffs at my words as if they are beyond the realm of ridiculousness.

"So with all the time and resources at your disposal, why are you yet to cure yourself? Have you actually really tried?"

"Oh, you have no idea what I have done to try and find a

cure, the lengths I have gone to, the endless line of girls I have paid to kiss me and worse – hoping that there was a grain of truth in those fairy tales."

"Maybe you just haven't found the right one yet."

The sound he makes is pained, like an injured animal taking its last breath. "Or maybe I am not worthy – I know I am not a good man. Maybe, despite everything, I deserve this curse."

I stare at the fabric for a long moment, wishing it wasn't there, wishing I could see him, take away his pain. "These girls you hurt, you didn't mean to, you were hurting yourself."

"No, I've always been a monster. I know what I really am."

"I've known scarier monsters than you."

"Perhaps, but you must remember that monsters are more than horrid looks and claws and teeth – monsters are born of deeds done – unforgivable ones."

"Are your deeds unforgivable?"

"Are your father's?" he volleys back and I have no answer, or maybe I do and I can't voice it. What has this man done to believe himself unforgivable? His chair scrapes behind the curtain. "Goodnight," he says, sounding less like the confident, arrogant man I have known and more like a broken old man.

"Am I not reading to you this evening?"

There is a short silence as his steps halt, and I wonder if he is looking at me over his shoulder. "We've both heard enough stories for one night."

23

DORIAN

"One doesn't intentionally to alter the truth, just enhance it and make it more memorable."— John Alexander

Two more days drag by like a wounded animal hauling itself to its final resting place. Jinx is a new kind of silent, like she's finally found her voice and is using it to put a barrier between us. She does her chores and eats her dinner. I haven't asked her to read for me and I feel her frustration simmering beneath her skin. She wants her work, but I want to give her back what I have taken. I want to give her so much more than I have a right to ask for.

She is a fucking drug and they don't have rehabs for addictions like her, but am I willing to give her up? Go cold turkey? Watch another man come into her life and give her everything she deserves? I shake my head at the invasive thought, pushing it out. I don't want to think of another man or anyone else at all that may dare take her from me, and if I look at myself and ask what it is that I really want from Jinx, the answer, despite glaringly obvious, is ridiculous.

Monsters don't get what they want, and any attempt would disrupt the perfect fantasy world I should not have been constructing in the first place, yet as I place the last piece of pie in my mouth I am already constructing a new plan, one that I know I shouldn't, but I'm already in too deep. And I plan on taking her with me.

"Join me in the lounge when you're done," I say and get up, leaving her there to finish her dinner.

She comes in and edges her way around my chair, finding me seated. Her weight rests on her back foot as if she is ready to bolt out of the room and standing still might commit her to stay. After our last encounter, I can't say I blame her.

A stack of her papers lie face down under my arm and her eyes flicker over to them before they search the veil that hides my face.

Always searching.

"I'm here," she announces, like I can't see her, and I bite down the sigh that wants to slither from my mouth. I don't want to spoil this.

"Before we start, I have a question for you."

"More questions?"

I ignore her. "If you could have one wish, what would it be?"

She bites her lower lip and sinks into thought. I wait. Her nervous energy flickers in the room like fireflies. "I'd wish to see my mum just one more time."

I nod. Of course, I should have guessed.

"What would be yours?"

Her question surprises me. But the answer is easy. "To be the best version of myself."

"And what is that?"

I ignore her and the sudden need to pick at my scalp.

Maybe I'm no longer sure myself. "Come sit down," I tell her and watch as her eyes roam the room.

"Where?"

"Over here." I nod to my leg.

Her mouth falls slowly open, and I can see her fighting to swallow down whatever protest is lodged in her throat. It's sweet, but as always, futile. I know she will do what she is told; she wants her work back. The thought pinches my skin when I remind myself that is all she wants.

When she keeps standing with her mouth open, I help her out and tap my lap. "It's not a difficult task." My tone has her face twisting in that way it does when I piss her off. A ghost of a smile flickers across my features. I like her angry. Fuck it, I like her every which way. The thought makes me shuffle in my seat even as I try to remain calm. The reality is, I have asked her to do way worse and yet here, at this moment she is more hesitant than ever, she has no idea that in five minutes from now I could be doing just that.

"What... I don't understand." She keeps staring, confusion splayed on her face like a painting gone wrong.

"Not that hard, Jinx." I tap my lap again and my voice is raspy but soft, like I'm actually trying to be nice.

She swallows, her throat bobbing before she makes her way to me, stepping around my knee and wedging herself between my legs before sitting on my left thigh, back straight and hands laced on her own thigh as if I was a church bench. It's amusing and I find myself smiling again. It lasts all of a short second as I realise it's just another reminder that she feels nothing but fear and discomfort around me. But I'm in too deep. I want this.

I lean forward and feel her tight muscles compress further as if she is getting ready to shoot out of my lap and into the air. I grab the stack of papers and sit back into my chair letting my skewed back adjust into the specially made curves and bumps that make sitting bearable.

I glance at the words and start to read; a story about a man and a Genie. Her head turns towards me, but her body is still strung tight. I read for a minute then another, her eyes flicker about and her coccyx digs into my thigh bone with each of her slight uncomfortable movements.

"Relax, Jinx," I say and continue reading her story. I don't look up and I have no expectations. Slowly, the tension in her body begins to melt, gentle uncertain movements that slowly see her head settle into my shoulder and have her legs draping over mine as her spine and hips curve to settle more closely against me. Without thinking, my left hand slides around her waist and hangs there, my fingers drawing lazy circles on her thigh, and only the sound of my thundering heart and my words fill the room.

"What are we doing?" she interrupts. Of course she wouldn't be able to sit through this and enjoy the moment.

"I am reading and you are interrupting." She pouts and her head lifts from my shoulder as she faces me.

"You know what I mean. What is *this*?"

I inhale a long breath, my eyes searching her brown ones that constantly flicker and narrow and try to see beyond the veil that separates us. "Would you rather I bend you over and fuck you?"

She gulps, her eyes widen for a second and she shifts on my lap, her thighs squeezing together for the briefest of seconds before she drops her head once more and remains quiet. Her reaction has my body ready to pounce and a smile slithering across my face, but I promised myself this. I continue reading her words to the room and she reads along. Every now and again my arm comes around her for a moment as I flip through the pages, and in those moments while she's in the circle of my arms, my mind plays ridiculous tricks that fuck with my reality. All of it feels way too... intimate. Except none of this is. It's not real. I corral my thoughts and finish reading.

The room falls silent for a long minute as she remains nestled against me, her body warming mine hotter than the burning fire. And that's when I kiss the top of her head. "Thank you." She jerks away and once more tries to search my face, her eyes flickering around. I hand her the papers and plant my feet down to stand, making her slip gently off me.

I can't help but slip my hands around her and glue her body to mine. My hand glides along her spine and closes slowly on the back of her neck, giving it a little squeeze. I delight in the way her mouth falls slightly open and she gasps at my touch, but more so the look in her eyes as they keep searching for mine. I know what desire looks like, lust, need, and I see them all in her eyes – for a second I have an aching to reveal myself to her, to take her there like the beast that I have become. But I've seen how my face drains any sense of hunger from the faces and bodies of women and so I release her.

"Get some rest, Jinx, you return to school tomorrow," I say as I leave her there and make my way to my room, where I slam myself against the door, fighting the turmoil that wrestles inside me.

24

JINX

"If history is written by the victorious, what if the victors lied?" — Michael Duncan

y eyes are bleary, and I scratch the sleep from them, feeling as if I am rubbing salt into my eyeballs. I am yet to consolidate what I feel for Dorian and how it felt last night to just be resting in his arms as his raspy voice sang out my words in a broken melancholy melody. Hearing him like that without the anger and formality is thawing something inside me, and resting against him, feeling the warmth of his body against mine, the beat of his heart, has me questioning everything all over again.

A short stack of papers lie on the small bedside table and a shiver wracks up my body. He's been in my room, watching me... again.

I drag myself from bed and start my routine; wash and change, grab breakfast, then grab my car keys. Winter break is over and I can't wait to get back to class, get back to the land of the living and away from the monsters.

I make my way to the grand garage where a host of luxury cars stand in a gleaming line and get into my tired Subaru. I slide the keys into the ignition and it sputters and spits but doesn't turn over. I try again and a third time. The car won't start.

I hit the steering wheel with both hands and climb back out, trudging back into the house. So much for freedom.

"Dorian?" I call out. I feel his presence, but all I get is silence. "Dorian?" I try again. His name echoes down the hall and bounces off the cold walls. When he doesn't show up, I storm upstairs to my room where I throw my bag down on the bed and grab my phone, calling the office to apologise for my absence.

I'm assured Professor Burns will be informed and my stomach does a long slow roll.

I do my chores, my body moving as if on automatic pilot, same movements same parts, like being conditioned for something. When I am done I clean up and head to the library. Dorian is not there. It's unusual and a shiver runs inside me. I search the house to find it empty. It unsettles me.

By the time dinner comes around I'm a jitter of nerves. Confusion hums inside me all day, a restlessness like I've swallowed a nest of bees. Something doesn't feel right, something has tilted, changed, shifted, I just can't put my finger on it. Or maybe I don't really want to.

"Good evening." His voice slices the silence in the room, and my heart jolts. "Did you have a good day?"

"My car didn't start; I've been stuck here all day."

"I'm sorry for your inconvenience."

"It *was* inconvenient! And I called you and looked for you." I sound like a whiny kid, but I don't care.

"I'll have Victor take a look at it first thing tomorrow morning."

"Thank you." My irritation is palpable. "Where were you anyway?"

"Things had to be done."

"Things?"

"I had my own chores to complete."

"What sort of chores?"

Our conversation is interrupted by Victor and the dinner dishes. He places them silently down and leaves the room. I start eating. My body famished.

"After dinner, I'd like you to join me in the lounge," Dorian says. "I have a surprise for you."

"A surprise? What is it?"

"Well if I told you, it wouldn't be a surprise now, would it?"

I scrunch my nose and grind my teeth. He's right, but I know curiosity will eat at me as I eat my dinner. They say patience is a virtue, but it's the worst one.

Slowing down, I chew each mouthful longer than necessary. The idea of a surprise from Dorian has my body quivering. A sliver of fear entwined with desire creeps inside me.

Dorian chuckles at my antics. Fuck him. He shouldn't have said anything. I chew the tender chunks of beef from my stew, wondering with each bite what the surprise might be. With each bite I feel the wetness pool between my legs and I squeeze my thighs tightly together.

"I'll see you when you're done." He stands, the fabric shimmers and he appears. I hear the amusement in his voice as he lingers for a few beats, and I feel his eyes as they travel the length of my body.

I do my best to ignore him as I keep chewing the tender meat that has melted in my mouth long ago and is now nothing but a tasteless chunk on my tongue. I swallow only when he leaves the room.

The rest of the food is forced down my throat. The process is somewhere between pleasure and discomfort, much like my relationship with Dorian has been. I push away from the table and make my way to the lounge.

My legs tremble as I walk – a surprise, he said. I suck in a long breath and let myself in. The room is empty but for the furniture and burning fire. "Dorian?" I call out his name to the room as I slowly make my way inside. I'm greeted with the crackling wood of the fire and nothing else.

I round his chair and that's where I find it; a stack of papers lie neatly on his chair. I take two tentative steps and find the rest of my stories. They are intact and full and mine. I look around the room, searching, waiting, but there is nothing but empty space and a strange sinking sensation in my stomach. Why the hell do I feel so disappointed?

Trudging up the stairs, I feel my confusion turn into anger, and instead of turning left towards my room, I turn right, towards the forbidden place in the house; the last place where boundaries still exist.

His door is heavy set and thick wood and I pound on it. "Dorian!" Of course he doesn't answer me, not the second or third time either. "Fuck this," I whisper to myself as I push the door open and step into his room.

For a split-second, I stumble in the all-consuming darkness, before my eyes slowly begin to adjust. In the barely-there light I can make out a shattered mirror. It sits in an oval wooden casing that leans against the far wall. A four-poster bed sits in the middle of the room surrounded by an ocean of shards of broken furniture – evidence of his broken life.

"You're not supposed to be in here." The hiss is angry and broken and my head jerks around, searching.

My heart smashes against my rib cage as I search the room finding nothing but dark corners. "What is this?" I hold up my papers.

"The rest of your work, our deal is done. You can leave in the morning once Victor has taken a look at your car."

A small cough leaves my lips and my body deflates. I don't want to admit it, but I know exactly why I don't want this to suddenly come to an end. "You can't just..."

"Just what?" His raspy voice is suddenly closer and I whirl around just as the door shuts behind me, plunging us into darkness. Hands clamp around me and I'm off my feet for a split-second before he slams me against the wall, his body pinning mine, looming, overbearing. "Just what?" he repeats and it sounds like a savage threat.

"I... you..." There are so many words. "We have a deal."

"I'm ending it, it's what you've been wanting for a while now."

"And if it's not?"

That has him stilling against me. "Then it should be," he whispers and breaks away.

"You can't decide that for me. You can't control everything."

"What do you want from me, Jinx? I've given you your work, I've given you your freedom, *I'm saving you*, just go."

"I want to see you."

"I can't."

"You won't," I throw back at him and his body advances towards me till he's pinning me again.

"I *can't*." His frustration is palpable, and I move my hand up towards his face. I want to see. His hand closes around my wrist and he snaps it away, holding it above my head.

"You don't know what you're asking for." His finger traces the line of my collarbone and tucks in underneath my chin, coaxing my face up.

"Show me..." I whisper, sensing his tension. It bounces off his dark heart which thumps wildly in his chest.

"Do you trust me, Jinx?"

I tip my chin. It's not a yes but it's not a no either.

"You'll need to cover your eyes."

"No." I glare at him.

"And bind your hands," he continues, pretending not to hear me.

"No. I want to see you."

"No." He pulls away from me and unbuckles his belt. He lets it slide slowly between the loops before he holds it tightly in his hands. "Take off your clothes."

I shiver at his command. And that's what it is, not a request. My heart quivers. What have I done, walking into the monster's lair? I swallow hard.

A shudder rips through my spine as I track his long broad body, always covered with heavy unshapely clothes.

My heart trips. I swallow hard and my shaking hands grab the hem of my shirt. I whimper as I pull it over my head and let it slip down my arms. The fabric evaporates as he snatches it. My hands shoot across my body, one covers my breasts the other my belly.

"Don't hide from me," he whispers.

I let my hands fall away. As he steps closer to me, I can feel the weight of his eyes through the veil as he drinks me in. It's intoxicating and thrilling all at once. My body wars with itself. But I have no time to think as his voice slices through my thoughts.

"You're not done." His gloved finger grazes my back, leaving a long harsh mark that stings.

I'm torn between his demands and my better judgement and my fingers slip into the elastic of my underwear. I let them slip off.

His silence grips me around the neck and squeezes till I can barely breathe.

"On the bed." The hesitation of a few moments ago has fallen away and given way to a husky demand.

I sit on the edge, then lie curled up in a ball.

"Let me see you." His voice is hot chocolate sauce dripping on ice cream.

"No," I throw back his own words.

The bed dips as he comes to sit beside me. "I want to see you," his raspy voice whispers in my ear, and I jerk from the warmth of his breath. His knuckles sweep my cheek and chin and travel down to my shoulder where he nudges gently, ever so gently.

He follows the length of my hands along the dip of my hips and slides along my naked legs where he draws out my ankles. I allow him this movement, stretching out my legs.

My head spins as I let him uncurl me, lie me bare on my back as my resistance melts to surrender. And then his hands are gone, only his erratic breath fills the room as I feel his eyes rake over my body.

My fingers grab the sheet and clench the fabric tight, fighting every urge to cover up, to hide myself.

"Dorian..."

"Do you trust me?" he asks.

I nod because I can't speak. He grips my wrists and slips the belt over them then tightens the hold before looping it through the headboard. He tests the knot a few times before he releases me.

With a feather-light touch he traces the line of my right cheek down along the tensed muscles of my throat to my collarbone and down between my breasts. I squirm under his touch.

"Shhhh." He pulls his hand away. "You're beautiful." He sounds almost disappointed, like he didn't expect it.

"I don't think I am," I whisper, my mouth so dry it's hard to talk.

"Because you're looking in the wrong places."

"And where are the right places?"

"Places where my hands can't touch, and only my words can reach." He stands as he says it and takes my shirt, the one I removed and sets it over my eyes. He fastens it around my head, covering my eyes. No matter how much I turn or squirm, the fabric remains. "Don't try to remove it." It's a warning. And I still, though my thighs clench tightly together.

Silence. Heavy and thick and it forces my breath out in short sharp pants. Anticipation crawls along my skin. *'Do you trust me?'* Can I? He's been so cruel in the past, giving so little and hurting so deeply. Leaving behind dark empty spaces where my emotions were left to echo. They scream for him. I swallow. Dorian is not a good man. He will take what he wants and give nothing back.

But before I can say anything, something touches my ankle. I snap it away but a gentle hand wraps around my ankle and pulls me back.

"Shhhhh," he coos as his light touch travels up my leg and back again.

Painfully slowly his graceful fingers trace my body, leaving behind blazing trails of want. Goosebumps erupt along my skin and my nipples harden and ache with want. The blindness intensifies every touch, making my skin feel alive. Like it's separate from the rest of me. I whimper as he touches everywhere but the places I want him to. A long torture that plays with my sanity.

"Dorian," I breathe out his name and it sounds revenant. Like I'm talking to an angel and not a demon.

He doesn't respond. But the first touch of his mouth on my skin is like fire. The gentle kiss lands just above my right hip bone. I gasp at the feeling and have no time to think as the next one follows and then another. And I *feel* everything. Plump, warm lips.

He kisses every inch of my skin, again avoiding the places I so desperately want to be touched. Even when I arch for him he ignores me, kissing my neck and tracing my collar bone with his tongue, nipping at my navel and my ankles till he rips my legs apart and kisses my inner thighs. Bristles scratch my skin. And still, he skips over my aching pussy.

I groan, unravelling. A garment threadbare, my threads being pulled in all directions leaving me frayed. I don't know how much more I can take.

"Dorian..." I moan out his name, imploring. Begging.

I gasp at the first lash of his tongue. So unexpected. My body jerks and my hips roll. He groans, and I know he's had his first real taste of me. My body aches for him to have another. And he does.

His tongue swirls and circles my clit, and my fingers itch to touch him as I pull against my restraints. I feel his smile against my skin before his tongue assaults me again. He holds down my thighs, his fingers digging into my flesh as pleasure builds inside me. Whimpers rip from my mouth as my body quivers and tightens. A hand creeps along my navel and up towards my breast, the sensation painfully good. I arch into his touch and the light stroke sets my body on fire, tipping me over the edge. Pleasure bleeds into every inch of me. I cry out as it rips through my body. Dorian's tongue and hand tease and stroke and lick while I grind into him until the very last wave leaves me drained and delighted.

When he moves, I purr, hoping to be set free. An ache has set into my shoulders and stretches through my arms. But he doesn't free me.

His body crawls over mine and he takes a nipple into his mouth. He groans, sending shivers across my body. I arch and my shoulders scream, my breathing falters, but he doesn't care. He takes his time. His tongue, his lips, his teeth all pull and tug and taunt my aching nipples, till tears gather in my eyes and a new ache builds between my legs.

"Please," I beg him, suffering through frustration, seeking his body which has total control of mine.

"Do you like me kind?" His breath fans my ear as he lays a kiss on my shoulder.

"Yes." My pulse drums against my throat a second before his lips brush over my own and his tongue touches the seam of my lips and vanishes leaving behind a whisper of a taste. My taste. I lick my lips, and he groans before dragging his cheek against mine. His whiskers scratch my sensitive skin.

He rolls away and a soft cry bleeds from my lips, disappointment clawing at me, till he rolls me to my side and his body moulds to mine. My back to his chest. His chest hair tickles my back and his hands cord around me like chains. One slithers its way to my neck while the other slides down to my wetness desperate for his touch.

I expect it, and yet I whimper when his fingers slide into me. So easily. They swirl and his hard cock digs into my ass as he presses against me, making sure I know how hard he is.

"Is this what you want?"

I gulp and nod against him then shake my head. His fingers circle my clit ever so slowly, teasing, leaking tension into my body instead of relief.

"What then?" he whispers as he slides into me. "What do you want?"

"I can't," I gasp as he pulls his fingers out and slams his cock into me. His grip tightens around my neck till needles prickle my throat and I draw in a desperate breath.

"Tell me." His voice leaves no room for argument.

"I want you," I rasp as he slams into me again.

"You have me," he growls, and pushes deeper and harder, his fingers clawing at my skin as if to remind me.

"I want more." My harsh whisper is the last of my breath. Darkness fogs the edges of my vision and he releases my throat as he slams into me again.

"Always more..." He grunts.

My lungs fill with air and my body trembles as if it's found relief, but it's a cruel trick as his fingers circle my clit, his hand closes around my throat again and his cock ploughs into me. He consumes all my senses, weakening me, breaking me, tormenting me, making me his with every second. I drown in him. He's the darkness and the light. The air I crave and the choked-up mess he drowns me in.

"I want your face," I rasp between pounds. He steals my breath with every move, with every swivel of his fingers, every thrust of his cock and the ever-tightening grip around my throat.

"Why?" His guttural sneer slices my insides with icy shards.

"Because..." My voice falls away as the darkness touches the edges of my vision again.

He releases me again and tears prickle my eyes. Relief and air floods through me and a hungry desire to fall over the precipice grips me. My body is overwhelmed, overrun with sensation. It's too much, too big, all-consuming and still, he's unrelenting.

He's part cruel, part kind and both sides of him ravage me at once. His lies hurt, his omissions frustrate, but his body tells me the truth – he wants me to be his. In much the same way I want him. The admission has me relieved and nervous all at once and my heart trips.

"Why?" He drags me out of my thoughts with a violent slam and all my nerves ignite.

I'm so close my body quivers, my hips search for his. My body responds to him, desperately needing, grinding, seeking relief, his torment too great to resist. My head falls against his hard chest. He is stone, hard and cold. And yet heat travels inside me.

"I want to know what you look like when you're between my legs, and the colour of your eyes, and if they screw shut when you come. I want to know the shape of your lips before they devour mine," I manage between rasps. Finding it hard to think past the pleasure. I suck in a deep breath like it might be my last. "I want to know how you look when you smile."

He groans, his thrusts erratic now. His fingers stroke my clit. My senses reel and my breath halts as my vision darkens. He squeezes harder, pounding faster. The edge has never felt so sharp, so steep. And then with a final brutal slam he releases my neck. Air floods into my lungs and my orgasm smashes me to pieces. I come and draw air and my body is so overwhelmed tears slice my cheeks and my pussy grinds against him as he jerks inside me, burying himself deeper as I squeeze around him. My breaths are short, sharp and desperate and everything feels broken and helpless and yet relieved and fulfilled.

He holds me till the last shudders fall away, my erratic breathing settles, and my body feels like it might belong to me again – like gravity has remembered to pull it back down.

"Was I kind?" His raspy voice grinds against me as he pulls out. His hot cum coats my thighs and I relish the sensation. It's a part of him I get to keep as a souvenir, even for a short time.

My shoulders ache and my body throbs and everything

inside me screams. *Was he kind?* "Release me." I tug at the belt. My arms and shoulders burn with pain.

"Soon, lovely Jinx." Heat sears my nipple, and I realise he's clapped his mouth around it. I moan and tug against the belt.

"Dorian." My voice sounds foreign. Wrecked and needy. "Stay..."

I feel the mattress shift as he pulls away from me and everything grows colder.

"Can I trust you to keep the blindfold on until I am gone or do I need to send Victor to free you?"

The thought of Victor seeing me like this sends a thrill of chagrin across my body and I clench my thighs. "No. I'll keep my eyes shut, I promise."

"Once I leave you may remove your blindfold."

I nod.

"Your arms and shoulders will be sore," he says in a tone I haven't heard before. Like he cares.

"I'll be fine."

"Jinx..."

"I said I'll be fine."

The tightness loosens and I'm able to move my outstretched arms. He was right; they scream with pain as I bring them down.

I lie in wait for more. But there's nothing more but silence.

I wait. My body cools.

"Are you still here?" I ask the dark, knowing there will be no answer.

I pull the blindfold off, my body a wrecked, broken thing. I rub my legs together, relishing in the gift he left behind.

Rolling on my side I wince with the pain, my shoulders burn and ache. I take my time extracting myself from his bed. I don't know where he is or where my clothes are. Weaving my way in the dimness towards the door, I make my escape to my room.

||||

DORIAN

I watched her from the darkness, the way she lay there waiting for me to do... Something, anything. Comfort her, hold her, tell her a version of the truth, but I did none of that. I just watched as I always do, cowering away in the shadows, embracing the monster that has overtaken my body, giving it life – allowing it to claim mine. And as I watched her wincing in pain and collecting herself, my body ached for her and I found myself wanting nothing more than to climb back into that bed and make her mine again, hold her against me, feel myself inside her. But we both live in a fantasy land I've created in this home. The false security borne of isolation. She thinks she wants what I have to offer but we both know once I step out of the dark and fully reveal myself there will be no turning back, for either of us.

When she finally leaves and enters her room, I step closer to the peephole. She's not completely solid on her feet, she sways, and I wonder if it's from the pain or the exertion. I expect her to go to the shower but she doesn't, instead, she climbs into her bed and keeps my smell and cum on her body. My heart threatens to explode and I have a severe and sudden craving to go to her, to hold her, to keep her.

But I don't.

Her presence has shifted everything. The hopelessness has evaporated. I feel with her here there is a chance for me. For the first time in an eternity I have a real glimmer, a chance, hope that she will be the one to end me.

When she finally falls asleep, I slip into her room and watch her, wishing I could climb into bed behind her and pull her into my body, enjoy her warmth, wishing we could have a real future, wishing that maybe I was someone else and that I could have something real, deserve something real.

Instead, I kiss her shoulder and listen to her breaths change as she falls into a deeper sleep.

25

JINX

"The beauty and gift of truth, is that it is not dependent upon your belief in order to remain true" — A. Dragonblood

When I wake my bed is cold. I shuffle, feeling the throbbing twinge in my shoulders and neck. I rub my bruised wrists and curl up on the bed, my mind splintered with indecision. Dorian has given me an impossible choice and he wants me to make it for the both of us. But I won't till he talks to me, till he confirms what I think I already know.

I sigh and roll onto my back, staring at the ceiling and listening to the rain smash against the windows. It feels like it hasn't stopped raining in days.

'Do you like me kind?' His words quake inside me, flooding my body with heat. His kindness is not without cruelty.

I dress and head down to grab my usual silent breakfast

when I hear noises from the dining room. I stick my head inside and I'm surprised to see Dorian sitting at the head of the table. The large fabric curtain that has divided the room is gone.

"Good morning." I hear the smile behind his veil.

"Good morning. This is a nice surprise." My hands wave in the absence of the fabric.

He nods and I feel the uncertainty as he waits for me to sit down. "I thought perhaps after last night... it seemed... fitting."

I feel the heat rise to my face and burn the tip of my ears as my body remembers in an instant every touch, every kiss, every pleasure. I squeeze my legs together and notice the smallest of tilts in Dorian's head. He's watching.

"What about the rest of it?" I wave at his face and the warmth that radiated a second ago vanishes, replaced instead by a fierce coldness.

"Soon," is his suddenly curt reply.

"Okay." I look down at my scrambled eggs. "Thank you."

I eat in silence. He watches me, not touching his food. "You're not hungry?"

"I'll eat when you are gone," He almost whispers it but the implications rumble around us.

"You can just—"

"No I can't, you'd lose your appetite."

I heave out a long breath and push my food away. "So this is how it's always going to be?"

"Always?"

"You know what I mean, Dorian, are you always going to hide from me?"

"I have shown you more of myself than I have anyone else."

"But not all of you."

"Why are the parts of me that remain hidden so important to you? Could you not be with me without seeing me? Am I not enough as I am?"

"I want it to be."

"But?"

"It feels like your omission is too great, you are hiding something and it gnaws at me, I need to know. Stop hiding from me and tell me who you are."

"Why? You want to hear about what a strikingly handsome, sad little boy I was, and how my parents were never around so I grew up manipulating and taking what belonged to me cause I was so fucking good-looking no one questioned my motives?"

"Yes!" My heart smashes in my chest.

"Yes?"

"Yes, tell me everything. Show me all of you."

"Why?"

"Because I can love you." The admission takes us both by surprise. Can I really love him, or do I just want a ticket home, a way out? Or am I already in too deep? Does the monster behind the veil deserve the love I feel for him? "I'm not so shallow as to turn away from you."

"My face is not the thing that will make you love me."

"No." I take his hand and place it on my cheek. "But your face will consolidate the picture that I've drawn of you in my mind."

"Just keep using your imagination."

"I can't do that, even the blind get to see with their hands."

"I've given you that chance."

"Once, briefly, it wasn't enough."

"No," he says, his thumb tracing gentle circles on my cheek, his body impossibly close to mine.

I sigh and try for the last time. "I could love you as you

are. I don't have to see you to *see* you. I know deep down who you are, but your face could tell me so much more."

"Like what?"

"Like when you're truly happy. I want to see you smile, frown, worry. I want to know what you look like when you're content or scared or sad or *lying*." His hand drops from my face and he backs away from me.

"Trust me, even if I wanted to, I couldn't lie to you."

I sigh, not knowing what he means even now. "I want to see all the truths in your eyes, why can't you see, your face speaks a different language."

Dorian sighs and shuffles around the room. His fingers twitch by his side as they often do when he's uncomfortable or considering things. "Okay."

"Okay?" My voice rises a few octaves.

"But not now. Tonight."

"Tonight?" I breathe the word like it's fire. A wide grin spreads on my face and I clasp my suddenly sweaty palms.

He nods and I watch him leave. Adrenaline floods my tingling body and a rabble of butterflies takes off in my stomach, their wings flapping in time with my racing heart. *Tonight.*

||||

DORIAN

The day stretches like a long endless road that leads to nowhere. Of course, I could have shown her my face at breakfast, but then I might as well open the door and push her out. She has no reason to stay now, not when I've returned her work, but this last hook, her curiosity is surely to keep her here with me even if it's for a few more hours.

Agreeing to show her my face was a mistake, but I know I can no longer keep hiding. I showed the others, it's the final step. This is what it takes, this is the chance I need to take. If she's to love me, it must be *all* of me, just as I find myself loving her with all her quirky imperfections.

I look at my hideous face in the mirror and grimace for the hundredth time this afternoon. How can I show her *this* when I used to be so beautiful? I open the top drawer and grip the picture. The last reminder of the man I once was. He stares back at me, perfection captured for all of time on glossy paper. He smiles with perfect teeth set in his perfect mouth, a sharp jawline framed by perfectly styled hair. And the skin, flawless. The man in the picture is sublime in every way.

I throw it back in the drawer and slam it shut, examining my blotchy skin and crooked yellowing sharp teeth, the thinning hair and the scabbed bald patches which I can't help but pick. My eyes fall to the floor. Who can love a monster such as me? Love me enough to truly set me free?

I don the veiled hat and pull on the gloves. Ignoring the knots in my stomach. I leave my room and go wait for her in the lounge.

My skin tingles and the fire feels too hot. Sweat soaks into my hat and my scalp itches. I resist the urge to pick and dig and grind my teeth instead. The wood crackles and splits in the fireplace sending a shiver down my spine. Bones sound the same when they break.

I feel her before I see her and I spin to watch her tentatively walk into the room. Her face is taut and her shoulders stiff. Her anticipation is laced with fear.

"Hi." She gives me a tight smile.

"Hi," I reply, my voice sounding foreign.

We look at each other in silence, there are no more words left to be spoken.

She walks towards me, her small body seeming to shrink as she closes the distance between us. She raises her hand, slowly, like it's been set in slow motion. She pauses, her hand hanging in the air between us and breathing is near impossible, like all the air has been sucked out of the room.

Without warning her hand shoots up and she removes my hat. I feel exposed, vulnerable, naked, and her eyes lock onto mine for a second before she gasps. And stares. Frozen. Her eyes grow bigger and rounder and her body stills.

Fuck.

I turn away from her.

"Don't," she says on an exhale, and I meet her eyes. They're big and round and... scared?

But then she reaches out to me, her fingers lightly touching my jaw, tracing the contours of my broken face. Just as she did that first time.

She shakes her head. Small movements that she probably doesn't notice. I step back and out of her reach, grabbing my hat and setting it back on. I'm hideous and best hidden behind shadows.

"Don't." She's back at my side and pulls away the veil, watching my face. Studying my eyes. Her gaze running along my face.

Before I can do anything else she's on her tiptoes and her lips find mine. They're soft. Softer than I remember lips to be, and her tongue breaches the seam of my lips and swirls with mine. She tastes like dinner and promises. I can't help myself. My hands close around her waist, pulling her to me, gluing her body to mine while the other slides into her hair, bunching it in my fist. I pull her head down, deepening the kiss to give myself access to more of her. And all I want is more. But then I feel it, the familiar tingle, the burning that begins at the base of my spine and spreads like a disease to the rest of my body.

I break our kiss and push her away. "No!" I scream at the room, panic settling like a rock in my chest as the burn crawls under my skin. "I didn't lie!" I scream as Jinx looks at me in terror, her eyes large. She takes a step back as more pain drills itself into my body.

I collapse to the floor, my knees buckling beneath obliterating, white pain. As the first bone breaks and I howl, Jinx keeps staring, like she's frozen in place. I want to scream at her – to tell her to leave, to run, but she doesn't. She stands like a cement statue watching my body break and deform in front of her. My bones shift and my skin burns as if I have been stripped of it and dipped in alcohol. I no longer recognise my own voice as feral, agonised sounds bleed from my mouth, and just when the pain is at its worst, it dissipates like a fog off some terrible lake, and I feel myself on my back.

26

DORIAN

"The truth was only another mask, even if it was the best
fit, the closest to skin and all that lay beneath"
— Michelle West

Slowly I become aware.

First, of the silence.

It's a strange noise, silence. It's the absence of everything, and very peculiar. I listen harder. I can hear deep breathing, maybe it could be mine, the noise now a constant hum against the drowning silence. Then I feel it, a gentle warm hand against my skin and her voice filtering through the darkness.

"Dorian?" Her voice is gentle and terrified all at once.

I crane my neck. It feels stiff and hard as if the muscles have forgotten how to work. I strain against sinew and flesh and force the muscles to pull and grind against one another until inch by agonising inch my neck swivels toward the sound of her voice.

Bright light flashes across my eyes and I blink it away as it all but sears my retinas. My mouth feels dry.

I swallow – the sensation like cotton balls scraping my tongue. I roll it across my mouth and look at her face. Somewhere inside me, I feel an echo.

I notice then that I'm lying down – my head in her lap. My supine body feels still as if it has forgotten to move, like a piece of furniture coated by cobwebs and dust.

I shift and my body creaks. It's an odd and unfamiliar sensation, my body might be deformed, but it has always retained the strength of ten young men.

As I lie on the floor, I exhale a long, drawn-out breath – like it's been caught inside me for far too long – it feels odd, expelling the air out of my lungs as if my body is deflating.

At the thought of my body, I become aware of it, and everything feels – different. Like I've awoken from a long dream and am still trying to grasp what's real and what's not, what is tangible and what's not.

"Dorian?" Her voice cleaves through my thoughts as her hand brushes along my cheek, and that's when I feel it, the pain.

An undercurrent of discomfort buzzes inside me. My joints scream at me. My fingers begin to ache, a twang of sensation, burning and slow like coals under a pile of ash. My bones creak and clang. Pulling and straining against my skin. I lift my hand to my face, wanting to confront this new pain. But what I see has my heart smashing against my rib cage.

I study this strange hand. Bony and scrawny, the greying skin stained with brown spots and deep blue veins like rivers under the surface. Purple stains and yellowing fingernails.

The hand belongs to an old man, a very old man, but that can't be me. I stare at the strange limb, resisting the idea that it could be mine even as I turn it back and forth, studying the skin, the bones, the slight ache in my wrist as I twist it.

I bring the hand up to my face; cold fingertips rip at my saggy skin. I frown as I map my face. It feels foreign, different. This face doesn't belong to a monster, but it's neither the one of the young man I left behind in that elevator. My body feels like a corpse, heavy and empty.

I roll my tongue in my mouth, trying to push down the rising bile and find the missing tooth. I don't remember losing it.

"Dorian?" Her voice rattles through my thoughts once more like thunder, and my eyes find hers. There's wonder there and terror, and she looks as if she is staring at a monster. I realise that of course she is.

I try to lift myself and scramble away, but my body collapses beneath me – like it's new, like it's learning to move all over again.

"Take it easy." She reaches out to me, but I scramble back again, flailing like a baby on tiled floor.

"What the hell is going on?" My voice croaks and breaks.

"We did it." Her voice is a whisper, like she's worried it might break me, but the look in her eyes is the thing that scares me most.

"What did we do?"

"We broke your curse," she says, and my heart shivers at her words.

I look at my hands. They belong to an old man, not to me. It can't be. "No."

"Yes." She crawls a little closer.

"Stop! Don't come any closer."

"Dorian."

"No!"

She ignores me as she always does and her hands close

around my face. Her lips brush mine as if I'm still the same man I was ten minutes ago. But I am still under her touch, under her spell.

"This changes nothing," she whispers as her eyes search mine, but we both know that it does. "Let me help you."

Jinx calls for Victor, and when he arrives it seems he has aged fifty years in an instant. His face is marred in deep wrinkles and his once lush black hair now a white wave. Together they guide me to my room. The broken dishevelled mess bleached in darkness haunts me.

"Rest," she says as she pulls the blanket over me and kisses my forehead like a child.

I close my eyes. Maybe when I wake up this nightmare will finally be over and I can go back to being me.

27

DORIAN

"What is too absurd to be believed is believed because it is too absurd to be a lie." — Robert Jordan

I sleep and wake in a daze. Jinx is always there when I wake. She feeds my feeble body and tucks the blanket around me before I fall back into a dark oblivion. But today when I wake, there is strength in my body. It hums.

I push myself from the bed and sit on the edge, searching the darkness. Jinx isn't there and relief floods me. The darkness has hidden the truth. But I can no longer escape it.

I weave a path to the bathroom through shards of furniture and the remains of a broken life. My hand freezes at the light switch and I suck in a few breaths, preparing myself.

Light floods the bathroom as I finally find courage and step inside. For the first time in days, I see my face once more. But it's not my face, not the one I have been staring at for years. An old man stares back at me. In the reflection, I find parts of my younger self – the eyes, the sharp jawline, the slick black hair now wispy grey – but it is marred in wrinkles and folds that only time knows how to embed in a face.

There is a scream from deep within me that forces its way from my mouth as if my very soul has unleashed a demon – and as my fists clench and my teeth lock up, resentment already starts to grow inside me like an insidious tumour, and I know that she has cursed me all over again.

||||

JINX

He hasn't left his room in seven days. Despite my pleading and begging, despite me telling him I never cared for his appearance, he will not come out – determined to remain barricaded behind the safety of his door and the cloak of darkness. It's like nothing has changed, although we both know everything has.

"How are you feeling?"

"How do you think?" He sulks in the bed, not looking at me.

There are so many things I want to say to him, but it seems his stubbornness has nothing to do with his curse.

"I have something for you. There." He points to a thick envelope sitting on the bed stand and I pick it up. He holds up his hands. "Not here, not now."

Nodding, I tuck it next to me as I go back to sit next to him. "Please come out today, we can have dinner together –

it's at six." I try to make light of the situation, but he grimaces and looks down at his hands as if he still can't believe they belong to him.

I reach over and cover his hands with mine, but he pulls away from my touch. I sigh. "Things haven't changed for me."

"But everything has changed for me."

"But why?"

He scoffs at me. "Don't!"

"Don't what?"

His sigh is long and tired like all the years that have shown up on his face have caught up with the rest of him. "Go home, Jinx."

"This is my home."

"You can't stay here, you don't understand what needs to be done."

"What are you talking about? We've broken the curse, we did what you wanted..."

His laughter is bitter and agonised and a tendril of fear slithers inside me.

"Go home, Jinx," he says again.

"But I am home." I put a tentative hand on his skinny leg, all the muscle eroded away, leaving only greying skin hanging from the bone beneath his too-big pants. He flinches away from my touch.

"No. It's never been your home. I forced you to be here, I forced myself on you. I took advantage of you and I liked every fucking moment of inflicting that on you, and now I'm done with you, so just go."

"*Done* with me?" His words sting the deepest part of me.

"Yes." His eyes lock onto mine and he waves his hand at me as if he is shooing a fly.

"Maybe it started out that way, but now... Things

changed between us. I know you feel it too." Tears sting my eyes.

"There is no *us*, there is no now, and the quicker you realise that the better – now get out of my house."

"Dorian."

"Get out!"

And just like that, he has broken me all over again. My heart croaks in my chest in desperate attempts to maintain some kind of order. His words echo deep inside me '*monsters are more than horrid looks and claws and teeth – monsters are born of deeds done – unforgivable ones*'. I shudder to wonder what else he has done.

I stare at the door for another short minute before turning around and leaving his room. I pack the few possessions I came here with, careful to leave behind anything he may have given to me. Throwing my bag over my shoulder, I take a final look around the room that used to scare me so much, that I'd hated, that I've now grown to love just as much as the monster who lives next door.

I stand at his door with my bag slung over my shoulder and a fractured heart that thuds a heavy beat in my chest. "I'm leaving," I call out to the shape in the bed but get nothing but silence. I've tried, I've implored, I've explained – but I'm not going to beg.

"I guess it was an asshole curse after all!" I turn around and leave.

||||

My apartment holds a chill that wraps itself around me like an uninvited intruder. It's clean and meticulous and, thanks to Dorian, my rent has been paid for a full year.

I throw my bag on the floor and collapse onto my bed. It

feels uncomfortable, unfamiliar – empty. I lie there for a long while, revisiting my conversation with Dorian, the anger in his voice, the desperation in mine, the thud of my heart a soundtrack to our end.

I lie there, my gaze searching the empty walls and roaming into dark corners as if parts of him are still hiding there. I shuffle onto my side and my gaze lands on my bag, inside the thick white envelope he'd given to me.

I reach for it, my heart smashing against my rib cage as I tear it open. A letter and a picture fall out of the envelope. I examine the photograph first; a gravestone, dated but nameless, sits beneath a tree surrounded by lush green grass. I study it for a minute longer but it tells me nothing. Setting it aside I reach for the letter.

The handwriting is neat and rounded, black ink on pristine white.

Jinx

Getting to know you has been the greatest privilege of my life, and I wanted to thank you by giving you something you really wanted - your wish. I have been searching for your mother, hoping to reunite you.

A pit opens up in my stomach as it begins to churn.

I have found her.

I wish I could give you better news, but it seems someone else has found her first. I have attached the details of where you can find her.

I know it's not the reunion you were hoping for.

The rest of the letter falls from my hand as the truth of my mother's death surfaces like a fresh corpse over water. I had always held onto hope, and now he has stolen that from me too.

The tears come then, streaming down my face, my chest heaving with my sobs. My body shakes with each shuddering breath, and I feel the weight of my emotions bearing down on me. It's as if I have been carrying a heavy burden for so long, and now it has finally caught up to me. The tears flow freely, unbidden and unstoppable, wrenching from me in raw, desperate emotion, staining the letter, the ink blotching beneath them.

I cry till I have no more tears, till my scratchy throat aches and my chest feels hollow, and the world closes in on me.

28

DORIAN

"Truth is born into this world only with pangs and
tribulations, and every fresh truth is received
unwillingly." — Alfred Russel Wallace

The house stands silent and I wait in my usual spot, somehow expecting that despite my banishment and harsh words Jinx will walk through the door, squeak her hello and begin to work. But as the clock ticks away I know she's not coming.

It's well after lunch when I finally give up and trudge to the lounge. The house is full of reminders of her; my dining room table, the hall where I first convinced her to peel her wet clothes off, my library where I first took her, my bed...

I sit by the fire, the chair made for a monster with a twisted back – no longer fitted for a feeble old man – digs into my spine. I stare at the fire, my mind a pendulum of doubt. I could call her, I could apologise, I could tell her how I feel, how I *really* feel, but that would imprison us both all over again.

I have been here before; this is not the first time I have seen my reflection as human since that night with Eris, each time older and more grotesque. Each time reminds me that no matter what shape I take I will always be a monster.

The sins of my past, my selfish ways carved on my body, as long as I live I remain cursed. I will never be anything else and Eris was the only one to truly know it. Part of me wants to believe I have changed, that I can be selfless, loving, but my bones scream with the truth of my being. There is only one true end to the curse, only one cure – and only one person who can make that choice. Be selfless. All she has to do is love me enough to do it. I cannot do it myself. I have tried countless times.

My heart chugs slowly in my heavy chest and I draw in slow long breaths. Maybe if I slow them down enough it will stop beating. But nothing seems to slow my pulse, my thoughts keep growing like gnarled, twisted roots inside me.

Telling her the truth would make her a prisoner again, and for the first time in my life I am lying to myself and the lie shreds my insides. But it is what I deserve. All her stories painted a pretty clear picture – monsters don't get second chances, they don't get a happily ever after and they don't get to keep the girl, even if they love her.

Especially then.

I keep reminding myself that I did the right thing, I called myself out, and now I deserve my just rewards.

She doesn't understand yet; she will be angry and bitter, but I *saved* her. She is free, while I will forever remain a prisoner in my own body.

I made a choice, now I will live with it till my end. If it ever comes.

THREE MONTHS LATER

JINX

"Better a cruel truth than a comfortable delusion." —
Edward Abbey

The ceremony was lovely but took too long. Getting my degree has somehow tightened the noose around my neck rather than loosened it. I hoped with finishing university I'd have a direction, a purpose, but all I have is remnants of broken promises and hollow dreams. Professor Burns did send my work to a publisher he knows and tells me they are interested in working with me. I'm still considering his offer. I would love nothing more than to have my name plastered on a hardcover of loved stories, but at the same time, I'd have to sign contracts, reveal my identity and spill my truth. My fairy tales need to remain buried along with my secrets. I am a loose end and despite my mother's death, my father is still out there some-where, no doubt still looking for his lost property.

When my name is called to the stage, I walk across it, and despite everything, I am proud of myself – I did it, in spite of all the obstacles I had to face. My heart quickens with the memories and goosebumps erupt on my skin despite the overly spring sun.

I scan the audience – smiling, proud families – an array of joyful faces here for everyone but me. But then, I see it; the car. The door slams shut and Victor walks around to the driver's seat. Our eyes catch for a second, and I swear a ghost of a smile touches his lips as he nods and slips into the driver's seat. I think I see a shadow move inside before the car takes off. Dorian came to watch my ceremony? But still not man enough to have come and seen me face to face.

The thought of his name sends a shiver inside me, it ripples in anger and devastation as it makes its way through my body. I still mourn the loss of him, and I'm so angry with him for leaving me alone, just like everyone else.

A week after he'd sent me away I went back, hoping he would listen to reason, hoping he would hear my heart and realise it belongs to him, but when I got there he was gone. All of it – abandoned. Just like me.

||||

The bar is packed, the music is blaring. Not bad for a Tuesday night. I sit at the edge of the bar, running my finger on the rim of my glass. I shouldn't be drinking, but then again, why not? I have nothing but time and a useless degree. A celebration for one. Yay me.

I pull down the mini skirt that's been riding up my thigh and catch a pair of brown eyes staring at them. Eventually, they track up my legs, taking a momentary stop at my breasts before finding my eyes. "Take a picture, it'll last longer," I throw at her and she smiles before making her way to me.

She's stunning. Tall, with long sky-blue hair and piercing brown eyes with golden flakes. "Evening, Jinx," she says as she makes herself comfortable on the stool next to mine. A shiver runs down my spine as something eerily familiar about her strikes me.

"How do you know my name?" The sense of unease continues to wrap itself around me as I study her. She looks into my eyes and in that brief moment, a surge of inexplicable emotions overwhelm me – a mix of awe, trepidation, and a peculiar fascination as a vision of a stone mosaic surrounded by roses flutters through me.

"Would you like another drink?" She ignores my question, her tone playful, almost mocking.

"Eris?"

She winks at me and her chin tips forwards in a slight nod. "We have a mutual friend. Dorian," she says, and the awe that swims inside me turns into something else.

"He's no friend of mine," I manage through gritted teeth.

"Ditto."

I narrow my eyes at her statement. "What do you want?"

"The question is, Jinx, what do *you* want?"

I rub my hands over my face and shake my head. This woman is starting to get on my nerves with her vague questions and strange behaviour. She might be stunning, but she is clearly waving more red flags than a bull tournament.

"Look, lady, I don't know who you are, how you know me or what you want, but all I want is a quiet drink and to go home, so please leave me alone."

"Is that *all* you really want, Jinx?" Her eyes lock onto mine and she waits patiently.

"Who are you?"

"You know who I am."

I sigh. "Fine, what are you then?"

She gives me an enigmatic smile. Her presence here is

both haunting and captivating. "That is irrelevant, what is relevant is that I can give you what you want."

"And what is it that you think I want?"

"To go home."

"I just said that."

"Yes, but we both know which home you really want to get back to."

My heart stutters in my chest and my stomach coils. How could she possibly know any of that? "He's not there, he's gone."

"He will come back."

"How do you know?"

"Because I am going to give you a choice."

"A choice?"

She tips her head, a strand of hair falls over her eyes and she tucks it behind her ear, her brown eyes lock with mine and I see the gold flakes swimming inside. In that moment she seems surreal, ethereal. "You can have him, but you need to choose how."

"Why did you curse him?" My curiosity gets the better of me.

Her mouth twists. "He cursed himself by being the beast that he was."

"And now?"

"And now you can choose to be with him, or set him free and let the loneliness eat you alive." Words I've heard him use – their echo bites at my soul.

I take a long sip from my drink and let the alcohol sting my tongue and burn my throat. I set the empty glass down. "What do I need to do?"

"Choose. Choose which version of the man you would like. The broken ugly beast, or the bitter old man."

"That's not fair."

"There is a third option of course." She smiles at me, it's

easy and careless, and I search the bar for an ice pick. When I don't find one, I flag the barman down and ask for another drink. He barely listens as he stares at Eris; her smile stretches and her eyes glow, and for a second, I wonder how life must be for her. So easy, so effortless. She dismisses him with a wink and he goes to prepare my drink, his tongue all but lolling out of his mouth. It's vomit-inducing, and I realise that I do not wear jealousy well.

We sit in silence while I wait for my drink, the music blaring around us as Eris fends men away with dangerous looks and narrowed eyes. Tonight her attention is focused on me. I wonder how many male fantasies she feeds as she keeps her eyes locked on my face.

I drink slowly. My brain is swirling in a tornado of doubt. How can I possibly choose? How can I possibly know what he wants? And even as I think it, I remember.

'What would be your wish?'

'To be the best version of myself.'

I make my choice.

Eris nods and whispers unintelligible words into the universe. "Now go to him."

30

DORIAN

"And this is the forbidden truth, the unspeakable taboo -
that evil is not always repellent but frequently attractive;
that it has the power to make of us not simply victims, as
nature and accident do, but active accomplices." — Joyce
Carol Oates

I stare out on a miserable dark sky; the moon bleaches out some of the darkness and highlights the scattered clouds. Maybe it could have been beautiful, but without her, everything has become bland and ugly once more. I shut the curtain, sealing myself in darkness. It has become my friend again, a cold black silhouette casting a shadow over me.

I quiver.

My body shudders.

A screeching pain begins to build inside me. A pain I haven't felt since our kiss. *That* kiss. The one that sealed my fate. That changed everything. Again.

The pain slithers like a fire serpent inside me, leaving ashes in its wake, and my bones begin to break and shuffle like shifting continents, I fall to my knees and scream.

31

JINX

"Fear nothing but your conscience." — Suzy Kassem

I wait three days before I go. My heart beats in a wild frenzy all the way to his home. Excitement runs along my body, a strange comforting hum that lies beneath the surface. My car comes to a stop, the engine idles as I stare at the house, wondering what I might find when I cross the threshold. I turn off the ignition and step out, my heart slamming in my chest like a caged bird against golden bars. I make my way up the path to the house.

I knock on the door, expecting the hollow silence I have become used to, but instead, it falls open under my fist.

"Dorian?" I call into the darkened hall. Shadows dance on the wall while a fire burns in the lounge, the only source of light in the house. I'm greeted with silence as I take cautious steps into the lounge.

"Dorian?" I call, closing in on the hearth. The heat licks my face, and movement catches my eye. The shadows move in a jagged, angry dance. "I see you. Come out."

"What are you doing here?"

"What do you mean, I—?"

"What did you do?" His voice railroads me, anger swift and undulating like a tsunami knocks me back.

"I made your wish come true, just as you've made mine." It's hard to quell the bitterness in my voice.

"And what wish is that?"

"I wished for my mother, and you, you wished to be the best version of yourself."

He steps out of the shadows then, like a stalking beast, swift and angry he rushes at me, smashing me into the wall as he looms above me, his powerful deformed hand clutching at my neck, the long sharp nails digging into my skin. "And this," he squeezes, "is the best version of me?" His face twists in a furious grimace as he snarls, flashing his teeth. He didn't bother with the veil, with hiding, I see his true form. The monster that ran in the shadows.

"Yes." Tears spill down my cheeks. "Would you rather I wished you an old man?"

"I'd rather you would have let me die."

"But then I'd have lost the only man I've ever loved."

"I can live with that."

"But I can't." At that, he loosens his grip. His eyes narrow and latch onto mine as if he is searching for something. My doubts? My fears? I have none.

"Jinx... you have cursed me all over again," he grits through his teeth.

Anger prickles up my spine, and I push his immovable body. "I saved you, I love you."

He scoffs at my words, but I see the slight tick of his jaw and the quick fall of his gaze. "You *love* me?"

"Yes, just like you love me, whether you admit it or not. We broke the curse; we found a way out for you."

"And yet I'm right back where I started."

"None of it matters."

"Of course it matters, you have no idea what this is like."

I sigh. "Do you think I would be here if I cared? Choose *this*, if I didn't?"

"*This*?" he waves his hands over his body gesturing to all of it, "is what you want?"

I nod.

He frowns.

"This?" He gestures at his body again.

"Yes, all of it, I—" But before I can say anything else, his mouth covers mine, stealing the words from me, pushing away my protest, tilting my world one more time. It's greedy and needy all at once and when he pulls away his eyes devastate me.

I push him away, breathless, my lips bruised and swollen. "What are you doing?'

"Giving you everything you asked for."

"Kissing me again won't change things. Won't change you."

He runs a hand over his scalp where scabbed bald patches cover his skin, and he growls at me. "I know, but I that doesn't matter anymore, that's not what I want now."

"What do you want then, Dorian?"

"What I've wanted for so long, my freedom." He crowds my space, backing me into the wall, his large body menacing, looming above me. "I want to give you what you're asking for, —"

His words die in his throat and he searches my eyes, maybe for signs of deceit, maybe he still doesn't believe it all himself, maybe he's waiting for me to change my mind, to see him the way he sees himself instead of the man he is to me.

His lips brush mine, the touch a whisper only as his hot breath coats my skin. "I just need want you to remember that I tried. I tried to save us both, I tried to stop loving you."

"You love me?"

"I love you. I will always love you so much more than you will love me. I will always love you *enough*."

"Enough for wh—" He steps forward, stealing my breath and the heat from my skin, wrapping himself around me. Before I can draw in air, I melt into his strong form, his firm torso and the heart that beats within. His hands fold around my back, drawing me in closer.

My body shakes, needing to release the tension. Dorian devours me with his eyes, threading his hand through my hair, as if he can't quite believe I'm not part of an almost forgotten dream. His hand closes in my hair as he fists it and pulls my head back. When he kisses me it's sweet, gentle and totally unexpected.

He pulls away, his gaze searching my face. Maybe he's still waiting for me to change my mind, to reveal a hidden truth. When I don't, he takes my hand and places it over his chest, to his heart. It pounds wildly, in tandem with mine. I guess part of me believes that he's just excited, turned on. But up until this moment it hasn't occurred to me that he might be terrified, too.

We inhale each other, each lost in the moment and then his mouth slams against mine, devouring, all the tenderness vanishes, his hands roaming everywhere, exploring me.

When his hand goes to my breasts, every other part of me is envious; I want him everywhere all at once. I slide my hands down his back, along his spine, rutted with jutted, protruding bone, to his full, beautiful ass. I squeeze the flesh, wanting more as he works on my clothes, ripping them from me. They pool at my feet and I stand there exposed, vulnerable, his.

He grips my hands and pins them to the wall, his mouth

traces my skin, nipping and kissing as he makes his way down to my nipples. I moan as he takes one into his mouth, sucking and nipping at it, dragging it out with his sharp teeth. The lingering pain feeds my hunger and I arch into him, needing him to take my other side into his mouth, but he seems content to torment just one side, leaving the other needy.

I moan in frustration and feel his smile across my skin. He doesn't relent; his free hand traces a line down my belly and his fingers sink inside me. We groan in unison.

"You're so wet for me, Jinx." It's like he is almost surprised.

His mouth clamps around my tender nipple and his finger slides in and out of me rhythmically, his thumb circling. My knees begin to shake beneath me as the edge moves closer, hurtling towards me at speed, the building pleasure intense and savage. I moan for him as he assaults my body, "Dorian…" I moan his name, begging, needing, aching, and he pulls himself away from me, his fingers and mouth gone all at once.

"Not so soon." His eyes twinkle with mischief and lust and I have the urge to kick out at him.

"Dorian," I whine.

"Ssssssh." He releases my arms. "Bend over for me, Jinx," he hisses, and his voice is fraught with desire and darkness.

I turn towards the wall and do as I'm told, my hands clinging to the cold stone. I arch my back, giving the view he wants.

He stalks behind me, and all the hair on my back stands as he slides a hand along my back.

"So beautiful," he whispers, and I flush with heat and desire.

His hands run along my ass and vanishes before he lands a slap on my flesh. I cry out but don't move as another comes down on the other side then another and another.

My ass stings with reminders and my body aches for his touch.

"So lovely in pink," he says as he examines his handiwork. "Spread your legs for me."

I do as I'm told.

"More."

I spread wider, feeling completely exposed.

He slides in behind me, his hands digging into the sore flesh of my ass and massaging the pain away, reminding me of it all at once as his tongue lashes out and he tastes me. I moan at the feel of him, pushing myself up and out, needing more of his attention.

He ignores my need as he always does and takes leisurely laps at my pussy, slow calculated licks, like I might be an ice cream. He is in no hurry as my swollen clit comes back to life. I try to grind myself against him, force the pleasure from his tongue, but each time I do he stops and his hand comes down hard on my ass.

I whimper in frustration. I am so close and yet he holds me at bay, at his mercy, a prisoner all over again.

His pace never wavers, not even when my legs begin to shake and my moans grow louder and my need washes over me. I am so close again, I just need more; a little faster, more pressure. I need to grind myself into him, and just as I am about to spill, he stops. Again. And my world tilts, my beating heart jitters and my body screams.

"Dorian, please," I beg.

"Shhh, don't move." His voice is urgent, hungry, loaded with warning. My head drops as my body aches. He examines me, taking in my rosy ass and swollen pussy, my arched back and heavy breasts. He grunts, maybe in approval, maybe in content.

His hands stroke my back again, slow movements that have sensations running along my body. He circles my bruised ass cheeks and up along my back, down my arms, just feathering along the curve of my breasts, never touching. I purr in pleasure, in pain...

"You are so beautiful, Jinx." There is wonder in his voice as he speaks, like maybe he can't believe his own words.

He comes to stand behind me, his hard cock buried between my ass cheeks as his nails draw grooves into my back, slow trails of pleasure and pain. He slides his cock between my legs and starts to move, rubbing my sensitive clit, drawing moans from my body. His hands slither down to my breasts and he pinches my nipples, rolls them between his fingers as his cock becomes slicker with my juices.

"Fuck, Dorian." We both hear the desperate quiver in my voice, and still he doesn't relent, playing his cruel game with my body, making me depend entirely on him, need only him, beg only for him.

Pleasure begins to build inside me each time he teases, and the waves consume me. My legs shiver and my raspy breaths catch in my throat. Once again he stops me at the edge, pulling himself away, but before I can cry out my frustration, he has lined his cock up at my entrance and ever so slowly slides himself inside. I feel every inch of him as he sinks inside me to the hilt then holds himself there. I feel him pulsing inside me, and I moan as he grips my hips, holding us there.

"Fuck, you feel so good," he croons as my muscles settle around his cock.

He thrusts once, cautiously, watching his slick cock covered in my wetness as he does. He thrusts again, pounding into me with such ferocity my overwhelmed body falters and I steady myself against the wall, meeting him thrust for thrust as he hits my swollen clit with each one of his savage movements. And this time the edge is so close, my body quivers with need and desperation, and I know he won't steal this from me.

Pleasure builds inside me and I push against him, seeking relief as his body pounds against mine, his powerful hips smashing into me, his ragged nails digging into my flesh, his harsh breath warm against my skin.

The pleasure begins to travel down the curve of my back, with a blind striking motion. I live in this moment. It's this, only this. I've lost myself in him, I'm no one, I'm obliterated, there's no Jinx at all, there's only an ecstatic burning pleasure, and I am losing, lost, unmade.

I scream out my release. My body quivers and convulses with the pulsating waves of ecstasy that flow through me, and I seek him in the moment, needing him deeper and harder, needing him to grind against me. From behind me, his shrill shrieks escape his throat and end in a deeper howl as his own release finds him and he is inside me, pushing harder. We push and pull and grind like we are trying to become one monster, howling and growling our need and pleasure.

I find air in my lungs and the earth under my feet as slowly I come back down He pulls me to him, holding me in his arms. My face is wet with tears I didn't know I'd shed.

He pulls his head back and wipes the tears with a calloused finger; even this roughness brings more relief than my heart can hold.

I want to speak but all I can do is croak, "I love you."

His mouth paints a soft smile and he kisses the top of my head before folding me in his arms again. "I love you too."

He takes me in his arms, and I cradle into him. Dorian takes his seat and we sit silent by the fire as it licks our skin.

I nuzzle into him, his misshapen body curls around me. I am safe and content and I let my eyes fall shut.

||||

DORIAN

T stare at the face in the mirror, the disfigured half man she tells me she accepts, and I grab the comb. I gingerly brush over the few remaining strands, brushing them over the festering scabs. I ignore the fallen strands that remain embedded between the teeth of the comb. I look over my broken, bent body; it is young and strong but it is not human. It is not pretty and it is decorated with the marks she left on me last night.

She has professed her love to me. She was the girl that was meant to be, but now as she lies in my bed, I must face the ugly truth.

I slip back into bed and the warm sheets, then pull her to me. She lies in my arms. I've spent the night memorising every inch of her as she slept. Committing to memory every scar and dip, every dimple and crevice of her lovely body. She purrs and pushes herself against me as she wakes to my fingers drawing slow circles on her shoulders.

"Did you sleep well?" she asks, her eyes still shut, her back glued to my front.

"Well enough." It's not entirely a lie and I wait for my bones as they vibrate their warning.

"I could get used to this," she purrs, and my body lights up to the feel of her against me. She's sweet, and I do what I can to make these moments easy for her.

She turns to face me. Her fingers caress my face, feather light, following the contours of my jaw and spilling down my neck, along my chest toward my navel and back again. The way she touches me sends cold shivers down my spine despite the heat saturating my body. I bite down my grimace, trying hard not to pull away. She notices me stiffen around her.

"You don't like it when I touch you?"

"It's just..."

"Hard to get used to?"

"Or believe." Her brows dip.

"Believe what?"

"That you truly loved me enough."

"But I do."

"Then why did you come back? Why did you turn me into this?"

"Dorian? You wished to be the best version of you."

I don't know if she notices the knife in my hands or hears my words, but as I speak her eyes grow big and round, holding all the questions she'll never get to ask. I bring it down hard, sinking it between her ribs and into her chest. "Do you not see? There is no good version of me. The way to set me free is let me die, but you are too selfish just like the others, you don't love me enough to let me go, you want to keep me, to save your own heartache when all I want is to be gone. You are no better than them, you are no better than me."

There is a brief silence and a calm few seconds when she knows what has happened, but her brain is yet to grasp it. And then I see it, the inevitable comprehension. She reaches for the knife, her eyes growing even larger as she sees the blood. It oozes out of her, leaking in thin rivulets along the furrows of her ribs and pooling on the bed, soaking slowly into the mattress below.

Her hands wrap around mine, but they are small and weak and I easily grip them in my free hand and hold them above her head.

"What are you doing?" she cries out as her eyes dart around the room, looking for help that won't come.

"Ssssh, it's easier if you just let this happen."

"What are you doing? Let me go, stop this." She ignores me, as always. "Help!" she screams and I sigh. I guess I shouldn't be surprised – she's always been feistier than the others, less compliant, a fighter.

I smother her mouth with my hand and she starts to buck, her lovely breasts bounce around, splashed in red, the perfect little rivers now growing into a harsh steady cascade. The more she fights the harder her heart pumps, and the more the blood slithers out of her like a hot red snake. She tries to scream into my hand, her hot breath starting to slow as she keeps fighting, her legs kicking out at the air, her body flailing like that fish she made me throw back into the water.

A single tear rolls down her face and her eyes lock on mine. I wonder what her last thoughts are; has she realised how many times I had tried to save her? Is she regretting her choice? Is she wondering why it is so easy for me to let her go when she so selfishly wanted to hold on to me?

I watch the fight bleed out of her as the colour drains slowly from her face. Her breathing begins to slow and I watch her chest fight to rise and fall as each breath becomes harder, as her heart fights to keep her alive, killing her with each beat.

I remove my hand from her mouth, letting her suck in whatever air she can still get into her lungs. I always did like that she was a fighter.

"You know... what.... your problem.... is, Dorian...?" she pants through ragged, harsh breaths. I roll my eyes, I don't really care. "The only.... one that... will never love... you.... is ... you."

The words stab at me. But then what the fuck does she know about love, bringing me so close to the end just to snatch it away? It's when I don't react that she knows she has lost. Fear and despair sets into her eyes as she pleads with shuddering, broken breaths. My anger is swept away by a flood of red blood.

Her hands fall away now, limp by her side, her skin all but grey and tired as she takes a few last breaths. Her eyes, still locked on my face, glaze over as at last she dies in my arms.

I wait another minute, taking her in. She was, after all, kind of beautiful.

Then I call out to Victor.

He is at the door and I usher him inside. He takes in her naked body covered in blood and his eyes flicker from her body to my face. "The roses need tending."

He nods and walks over to the bed; she will make a lovely addition.

I leave him to clean things up and walk to my library where I near the window. Warm spring sun splashes its way inside and I rip my sharp claw across the four marks on the wall, digging into the wood and sealing the fifth line. I thought she'd be different, but like the rest of them, she chose wrong.

A WORD FROM JANE

This book has been three years in the making, rewrite after rewrite to find jinx, and Dorian's perfect story. It's been a long journey one that was carefully followed by Tracey Caldwell, who as always made me see through all he trees when the forest got too thick. Thank you, for all the encouragement, support and feedback. Thank you for pushing me back on the path.

To K – As always without your direction, comments and segues my writing will be no where near what it is or could be. You drive me to do better and get through the mountain… one day it will actually all happen… and no – no balconies! Thanks tyrant x.

Finally, thank you for reading, supporting my work and hopefully enjoying my words, my twisted worlds my broken characters! If you enjoyed the story, please leave a review and recommend the book to any friend you think would love this story. You will have my eternal love and gratitude.

Want to know more about the author and keep in touch? get snippets of upcoming books and have
a bit of twisted fun?
Come join me in Wonderland…
https://www.facebook.com/groups/wynterswinderland/
https://www.instagram.com/jane_wynters_author/

ABOUT THE AUTHOR

Jane Wynters doesn't quite know how to answer the question of "where are you from?" She's moved from place to place like a snowflake on the wind always searching for a safe place to land. She loves meeting new people and exploring new places. She loves reading, writing and conjuring new worlds from her imagination. Coffee is at the top of her food pyramid and she is fluent in three languages, her favourite being sarcasm.

Want to know more about the author and keep in touch?
Get snippets of upcoming books and have a bit of twisted fun?
Come join me in Wonderland.
Sign up for my newsletter

ALSO BY J. A. WYNTERS

Standalones

Guarding Gabriel

The Beverage Wars

Mai Tais and Goodbyes

Fractured

The Sweetest Thing

Losing Liam

Four Rooms

Liar Liar

Parts of Me Series

Spare Parts, Book 1

Fixed Parts, Book 2

Broken Parts, Book 3

Coming Soon...

Torn Apart, Book 4

Picked Apart, Book 5

The Fractured Fairytale Series

Beast

Wolf

Hunter

Dreamer